SECRETS AND SEDUCTION

a Dangerous Desires novel

SAHARA
ROBERTS

Entangled Publishing, LLC
2614 South Timberline Road
Suite 109
Fort Collins, CO 80525
Visit our website at www.entangledpublishing.com.

Ignite is an imprint of Entangled Publishing, LLC.

Edited by Candace Havens
Cover design by Louisa Maggio
Cover art from iStock

Manufactured in the United States of America

First Edition December 2015

ignite

To Ria Boulay, my partner in crime. Thank you for encouraging me, pushing, pulling, and generally lighting a fire under my ass until Andres and Moni's story was done.

Chapter One

"If you wanted me naked, all you had to do was say so."

Monica Vasquez's pulse spiked as she tried to glare. Andres Calderon's honey-brown eyes shone with a mischievous light, and he had the gall to give her one of his sexy, one-sided grins while he worked the buttons on his western shirt.

Oh, if only it were that easy, cowboy. I'd have you down to that hat and nothing else faster than that horse tossed you off. Heat crept along her cheeks as she willed the thought away. *For goodness' sake, Monica, he can't read minds. Now get a grip, he's a patient.*

She shifted her feet, wishing she could pull her gaze away. No patient had ever gotten to her the way he did. If luck was on her side, his eyes hadn't adjusted to the dark corner of the stable yet.

Andres pulled the dust-covered shirt out of his blue jeans with care. Her toes curled as the material draped open to reveal well-cut ridges at his pecs and abs. The rounded shoulders and muscle definition along his biceps only added to her unease. She desperately needed her white coat and stethoscope as a buffer, wrapping her in the protection and authority of her profession. The sleeveless white summer dress with a lavender flower print left her feeling vulnerable. Doctors were supposed to be unflappable when confronted by emergencies, chaos, or big, strapping, handsome cowboys with sun-kissed skin.

He winced, the pain on his face stripping away the teasing façade he'd presented since picking himself up off the ground. Years of training kicked in, pulling her attention from his tanned skin. She clasped his arm and directed him to the wooden bench along the wall. "Sit down for me." Her doctor's voice resonated in the small space.

"I'm fine, Doc." She inwardly rolled her eyes. Of course he was. What tough guy liked admitting to an injury?

"You took a nasty fall, Andres." Exhaling through flared nostrils, he folded his tall frame onto the worn bench and placed his hat beside him. She lifted her skirt to kneel, but he caught her by the elbow.

"Hang on." He draped his shirt at her feet before letting her continue.

Her lips parted, ready to tell him he needn't bother. She might be petite, but she was far from fragile. Yet the gallant gesture kept her from uttering a word. In the small town of Copas, Nuevo Leon, Mexico, manners long forgotten elsewhere were the everyday norm.

"Thank you." Her knees settled on the shirt-covered, packed earth. As she felt tiny stones digging into her skin even through the cloth, she was thankful for his consideration. "Lift your arms for me."

His back flattened against the wall. "No."

One, two, three… She kept time with the array of hoofbeats pounding across the arena, sending vibrations along her legs.

In all the time she'd known him, he'd never been difficult

with her. Teasing, joking, and testing limits, sure, but he'd never refused a direct request from her. "Andres." She adopted a tone. "Let's make sure you didn't break anything."

She hadn't seen him fly off the rearing horse, but she'd heard the spectators' collective gasp and the accompanying thud as his body hit the ground. As the town's resident, though temporary, doctor, she'd bolted to the scene, cutting through the crowd of spectators surrounding the corral. Her breath had failed her when she'd realized who'd been thrown. For a moment, time froze, as the noise of the crowd faded away, and the only thing she could hear was the pounding of her heart. Her entire being became fixated on the man lying on the ground at her feet. It had taken everything she had to step back and order the men to help Andres up.

"I'm *fine*, Doc." He folded his arms matter-of-factly. "It's not the first time I've landed on my…butt, and it won't be the last."

Men and their macho crap. She gave him a smile she hoped was ambiguous at best. "Do I need to bring in a couple of men to assist?"

"I spent the morning working horses, and the sun's hot enough to scorch fajitas on the hood of my truck." Fixing his gaze on a spot somewhere over her head, he grudgingly admitted, "I stink. So if it's all right with you—"

Of all the things to worry about, his first concern was whether or not honest sweat would offend her. "I can hold my breath for a long time. Promise." As a doctor she was used to all kinds of odors. A little manly man smell wouldn't send her running. "Now, I need you to pick up your arms." She encouraged him with a light tap to his wrist.

His gaze slid down to meet hers. "I'd really rather take a shower before you examine me."

She forced herself not to squirm as thoughts of his body, wet, slick with soap, nearly took her breath away. This situation was definitely *not* covered in med school. She drew in a deep breath, reaching for her patience. "If you cooperate, this can be over with quickly, and you can go take as long a shower as you want, how's that?"

The corner of his lips quirked up. "Maybe you can wash my back?"

Monica glared at him. "This is serious, Andres. You took a hard fall, please let me do my job."

He turned away, mouthing something she was surely better off not hearing, but did as she asked. "I learned to take a fall before I could wipe my nose." He hooked his hands behind his head and concentrated on a point above her.

She breathed a silent sigh of relief and tucked away the images of the two of them naked and wet. "Take in a deep breath for me."

His chest expanded to capacity. No visible damage, no further signs of discomfort caused by the fall. "You were on the ground, groaning and holding your forehead." She palpated the area, glancing at his averted face every few seconds for any telltale reactions.

"I had my hand over my eyes to block out the sun." Possible. The way he avoided eye contact convinced her this was embarrassment instead of injury. Either way, she continued her examination until she could live with his self-diagnosis of "fine." She lightened her touch as she covered his ribs. He twitched. Afraid she missed something, she checked again, concentrating on the spot she'd been touching when he'd reacted. "Besides, I got the wind knocked out of me, and I lost my hat…" His voice trailed off.

Try as she might, the man was impossible to ignore in such close confines. She spared a quick glance and did a double take. In the time she'd known Andres he'd been quiet and unobtrusive, then teasing and flirtatious. She would never have imagined him capable of such a tender, thoughtful expression.

Damn. He'd managed to scatter her resolve without even trying. In a heartbeat, she became acutely aware of how close they were. Him, taking up a good portion of the scarred wooden bench. Her, kneeling between his dusty cowboy boots while the zipper on his jeans pulled tight across an impressive bulge.

Her nipples puckered against the thin, unlined bra cups. *Noooo*. She licked the edge of her lips, needing relief for her suddenly dry mouth. This line of thinking would only lead to complications.

If she had any sense she'd walk out now and track down Dr. Treviño to take over. Her mentor was onsite, monitoring the local cartel boss's health while she filled in at the office.

"One of these nights we should try this again." His voice went low, strumming her heightened senses. "Only next time, I get to take your shirt off, too. Maybe take that shower... together."

Too late. Images of him peeling back her clothes flashed through her mind. Her gaze dropped to his mouth, caressing those full, sensuous lips like she'd been tempted to do so many times. How would his neatly trimmed beard feel against her bare wet skin?

Booted steps snapped her back to reality. "She's checking you didn't bust your fool head, you moron." Alejandro "Alex" Marquez, the ranch manager, said with disgust. "Not trying for first base."

"Bite me." Andres brought down his arms, rolling his right shoulder as he watched Alex place her heavily laden backpack on the bench beside them.

"Here's your pack, ma'am."

"Thank you." Moni got up, gently tugging Andres's torso forward to examine his back. She should have pulled on some gloves and stopped enjoying the feel of hard muscles.

Alex tapped his cowboy hat against faded blue jeans. "I've got to get back. I'll send Miss Lupe over to lend a hand."

"No need, Alex." The fiery sun tattoo below the back of Andres's neck caught her attention. "We're just about done here."

"Okay." He shrugged then turned on his heel and walked away, his natural gait a little stiff.

"When are you going to put me out of my misery, Doc?" Andres's throaty whisper, for her ears only, cleared a long, unused path back toward temptation. His palm settled on the curve of her hip, increasing the thrum that had started between her thighs. She stepped back, giving him an unexpected close-up of her breasts. He tightened his grasp while his lips parted for his heated breath to fan across her body. Openmouthed kisses… She bit the corner of her lip, unable to stop the shudder that ran through her.

The man was a walking contradiction. One minute he laid out his shirt for her, the next he was talking about getting naked. *Dios*, she'd gone way too long without getting up close and personal with someone. No one since…

From the doorway, Alex called out, "Take care not to get your skirt tossed around before you get out of here."

Holy Mother… Mortified, she stiffened, releasing her breath in a rush. What did these men think of her? Copas was way behind the times, but being alone with a man while examining him for injuries didn't mean they had a right to talk to her that way—regardless of where her thoughts had gone. She so needed to get out of this backwater little town and back to civilization. The second Dr. Treviño was free, or she got the call from Dr. Chavez, she was out of here.

Andres shook his head. "Doc?" He reached for her arm, but she twisted her wrist and pulled away, escaping with little effort.

Squaring her shoulders, she addressed him in her best

clinical tone. "*Don't* touch me," she ground out. Every part of her screamed to take those words back. "If you can't act like a decent human being, find yourself another doctor." She stomped around him and jammed her forearm through both straps of the Kevlar-lined backpack, stalking away as best she could in three-inch heels.

"Doc…" The announcement for the barrel races drowned out his words.

Humiliation, anger, and annoyance bubbled inside of her, making her throat tight. With jerky movements, she pulled the sunglasses from where she'd hooked them on the front of her dress. *Get a grip.*

She'd tried hard to stay neutral and unobtrusive. Cartel members could be volatile, but she'd kept to her tasks and managed to gain some level of tolerance. Andres had always been the epitome of politeness when he brought Dr. Treviño to check in at the office. Though if he found a moment alone, he'd try to tease a smile out of her. And it usually worked.

The wind blew her hair forward, whipping against her cheeks and tangling around her sunglasses. She yanked stray wisps out of her mouth.

Sometime during the last few visits his cute grin became a sexy smile, and his teasing had turned more personal… more intimate. What she'd hoped was a cold stare hadn't even slowed him down.

The wind gusted again, molding her skirt to her backside. Only the weight of the backpack she carried preserved her modesty. "Jerks," she muttered under her breath. "Sorry sons of—" She was halfway to the arena before Alex's words crept past her ire. Her steps slowed, and she dropped her head back to stare at the sky. *I'm such an idiot.* Alex could have been warning her that the wind could whip her skirt around. She bit the corner of her lip. After months of keeping her temper in check, she'd slipped at the wrong time. With the wrong person. A mistake like that could get her killed. Worse, she just might owe Andres an apology.

Ten minutes in the stands and Andres couldn't tell if his hair was damp from the hot shower or the afternoon heat. Today, he didn't envy the riders. They were covered in dust and baking under the scorching Mexican sun.

Andres's lips tightened. He scanned the crowd from behind dark sunglasses. Former friends, neighbors, and numerous aficionados from surrounding towns were enjoying the day's events. Several pretty faces dotted the stands, but the only woman he wanted was purposely ignoring him. She sat prim and proper, directly across from him, with another man. Simon.

Even as a child, Simon had been a spoiled mama's boy. He was over thirty and still at home, with his mother all but tying his shoelaces for him. He couldn't imagine the independent Doc with the sissy-boy Lupe had raised. Disgusted, he tore his eyes away. Unfortunately, things went from bad to worse.

Paloma Guerrero was making her way up the stands toward him while her three-man entourage lined the railing. Like her father, she did things her own way, regardless of whispers. Not that anybody was stupid enough to insult the cartel boss's daughter.

She sat next to him then scooted close enough that her hat brim brushed his. "Why are you sitting way up here, all by yourself?" The cloud of perfume couldn't mask the smell of smoke—and it wasn't cigarettes she'd lit up.

Andres leaned away, adjusting his hat. "Better view." Speaking of views, across the way, Monica kept her skirt tucked from the wind, her lean legs on display. He took full advantage of the cover his sunglasses provided to let his gaze trace the curves of her body, envying the white dress snuggled tightly against her.

Paloma pulled her hair over her left shoulder and gave him a flat-lipped smile. "When you're right, you're right." She stuck a neon-colored thumbnail into the front of her tank top and pulled. The material stretched out several inches before snapping back against her breasts. The action only reminded him of Monica kneeling between his legs, her sunglasses pulling the top of her dress open. Heat flickered in his gut as his thoughts spun quickly toward the things she could do there, things that had nothing to do with doctoring. He watched as Monica laughed at something Simon said and frowned at the unexpected stab of jealousy.

"Alex says you're a bull rider."

Alex talks too damn much. "A long time ago."

"I'd really like to see you ride."

He shrugged, refusing to take the bait.

Conversations with Paloma always involved tap dancing around certain subjects. Among them, the tenuous arrangement Dr. Treviño had set up for him with Guerrero.

Andres met Guerrero after Dr. Treviño had mentioned the Calderon reputation for handling horses. The drug lord had made him wait while he'd personally disciplined one of the men with a bullwhip before sending him off to recover in the bunkhouse. The poor bastard would live to carry the scars for the rest of his life. Guerrero had then walked up to Andres as if nothing had happened, his face flecked with the man's blood, and calmly offered him a job at twice what it was worth. When Andres nodded, unable to speak, Guerrero had roared with laughter.

"Now this is a man who understands consequences." He'd glanced once more at Andres. "Don't forget that...*cabron*." Andres hadn't. He trained the man's champion racehorses, tended to livestock, kept a low profile, and tucked away the money.

Across the arena, Monica still sat with Simon. The black and gray backpack was placed strategically between her knees and his. Something about the sight brought a smile to his face. At least he wasn't the only one she was dodging. "Dr. Vasquez had me sit this one out."

Paloma scowled. "You don't have to listen to her."

"She's a good doctor." He recalled the feeling of her hands, soft and gentle, sliding over his skin as she'd examined him. Was it his imagination or had her touch lingered a bit longer than it needed to? He just might need a follow-up with her real soon.

"Dr. Treviño is a good doctor. The best." She nodded enthusiastically. "Daddy said so."

Could be. But her father held an exclusive option on the good doctor's services, keeping him busy around the clock since he'd had some unknown episode a few months back. The rumors ran anywhere from him having heart problems to being a schizophrenic. Luckily Dr. Treviño had been present, but his fate had been sealed after treating Guerrero. "And he thought Dr. Vasquez was good enough to fill in for him."

Paloma leaned toward him, pressing her breast to his bicep. "You know, you're real smart."

Yeah. A freaking Einstein. "Your nose is starting to turn pink. I'll take you down to the guys so they can find you a better place to sit." He stood and offered her his arm.

She giggled, wrapping her fingers around his forearm as she stood. "You can take me *any*where you want." Sidestepping to the aisle, she slipped an arm behind him, shoving her hand into his back pocket.

His shoulders and neck stiffened. He should have taken his damn chances with a bull. Her fingers curled against his ass while he led her downstairs, supporting most of her weight.

"Da-mi-an." She reached out toward the guy at the foot

of the steps, pulling at his shirt collar to reveal the edge of a tattoo. *El Demonio*, the Demon, stared at him with freakishly dark eyes. Light skin and a well-defined widow's peak rounded out the perfectly earned nickname. From what he'd heard, Paloma put her keepers through a "rigorous testing process." Only those she was satisfied with remained in her employment. And Damian had been with her longer than any of the others. "Did you know Andres rides bulls?"

Andres acknowledged Damian with a nod as he firmly detached Paloma from his side. "She's starting to get sunburned. I gotta go back to work before Alex comes looking for me."

Damian slid his arm around her waist as Andres stepped back. "I got her." His brawny arms circled her hips as Paloma pressed against him. Sliding one arm over his shoulder and her other hand slowly up his chest, she tapped a finger on his chin, claiming his full attention.

"And did you know" —she tilted her head just enough to stare at Andres, smirking— "*his* daddy used to own this ranch?"

Andres's blood ran cold under the blazing sun. Damn Paloma and her bullshit games. Her petty attempt to remind him of his place could get him killed. Andres cautiously met Damian's gaze, wondering what would happen in the next few moments. If Damian couldn't get her under control things could get ugly fast.

For a few seconds the men simply stared at each other. Damian then rolled his eyes, assuming a long-suffering look. Giving Andres a small, quick head tilt, he reached up and grabbed Paloma's fingers, dragging her attention back to him.

"Chica, why you wanna play with the hired help when you got me right here, hmm? Let's go find some shade so we can…talk about this."

As Paloma giggled, Andres slipped around the pair and

escaped. He silently cursed himself for admitting to the bull riding. He should have refocused her on the action in the ring. As he turned and headed away from the crowds, he knew he'd have to be more careful around her.

His life and the future of Rancho del Sol depended on it.

Chapter Two

Andres tried not to think of it as hiding out, even though he'd been messing around in the stable since leaving the stands. Rayo nickered in his stall, bobbing his head, urging Andres to come closer. "You spoiled nag." Andres snatched a brush off a nearby shelf. "You think I'm only here for you?"

When he'd first returned to Rancho del Sol, he'd gone straight to the stables, thanks to Dr. Treviño. Riding enthralled him like no drink, drug, or woman ever could. Bull riding, once his obsession, was more of a guilty pleasure now. He knew the danger with either horse or bull, but Calderon men trained animals. They learned to ride before they could walk—Grandpa made sure. His earliest memories were of him in the saddle, learning from his elders.

Other memories crowded in, his mother teaching him to dance, his father's stories about building a dream home to keep his beautiful bride by his side. They'd moved out shortly after he'd left with Susana, his father concerned about the increasing cartel presence in the area. Instead of running the ranch, Andres lived in a cabin, looking up at the house he'd been born and raised in, while his parents' fears for the future played out in front of him.

Now he spent his days caring for the horses, getting them ready for the rodeo, which is what he'd been doing when Monica showed up, looking all pretty in a flowery dress. He'd been warming up Mota, following every twist of his bucking body. One minute his gloved hand held leather, the next he was boots in the air then ass on the ground.

He hadn't been thrown in years. Why today? Why in front of her? The only thing hurt was his pride, because he knew exactly what was going to happen. Sure enough, she'd run out to check on him, arriving just as he was groaning at his humiliation. He'd opened his eyes to find Doc's concerned face hovering over him—mistaking embarrassment for pain.

She'd issued orders like a little drill sergeant, and nobody had thought to stop her. The ranch hands had hauled him up, laughing, then sent them off to the stable. He had to admit things improved once they were alone together, and she was trying to get him out of his clothes.

The long-ago talk with Dr. Treviño had flown straight out of his head. But he remembered now. It included *look after her, wonderful young lady, treat her with respect*, and most importantly, *if I had a daughter*. Not that he'd ever be good enough. He winced, pulling his fingers against callused palms. But who could blame him? He'd been half naked, she'd been kneeling between his legs, her sunglasses tugging down the front of her dress…all his blood had rushed south, and he'd been struck stupid.

Over the past few weeks, she'd thawed from a perfect ice princess to greeting him with a friendly smile. He looked forward to that smile and worked for it when he had to. Earlier, he'd seen another rare flash of interest. He'd pushed—harder than he should have. Maybe not the smartest move, but he'd had his bell rung.

Then she had stomped off in those ridiculous shoes. Who wore high heels and a white dress to sit in dusty stands? But he sure enjoyed how the skirt moved with the swing of her hips.

Rayo perked up, his ears twitching. Curious, Andres leaned out of the stall and stopped short. Monica was heading his way.

She stopped a couple yards away, unusually quiet. "You didn't ride today."

"Nah." She couldn't know. Dr. Treviño hadn't let her attend the rodeo they'd had earlier in the season. He started brushing again, at Rayo's insistence. "I don't participate."

"But you're doing okay? No b—"

He snorted. "I'm *fine*, Doc. Go back to your date." The words stuck in his throat like dusty tumbleweed.

"He's *not* my date."

Good. He grimaced, annoyed at the stab of satisfaction that rushed through him.

Rayo mimicked his snort and stepped forward. Monica held her ground, and her skirt, but she did lean back a bit. The wind tossed her hair. "I...I hadn't noticed how windy..." She inhaled. "Andres, I wanted to—"

He didn't want a damn apology. "Happens all the time. My family believed it's the ghost of Uncle Rey, Grandpa's brother, blowing through here." His gaze went to the framed picture sitting under a weathered black ribbon. "He was older and took a tumble, breaking his hip."

"Rodeo?"

"Yup." He nodded. "The doctor warned him to be careful. At his age he wouldn't heal well after the abuse his body had taken. Didn't keep him from visiting with the ladies at a cantina one town over. One night he had too much to drink, missed a step, and lost his grip on the banister." Monica winced. "When he finally came to terms with the fact he'd never walk again, he took his life, right here by the entrance."

"*Dios mio*." She made the sign of the cross.

"Rey didn't have a family of his own. Grandma said the only girl he ever loved left him when they were young and never looked back. Guess he figured he had nothing to live for if he couldn't ride."

"You take after him?"

He shrugged, not wanting to consider what he would do if he couldn't ride anymore. "We're two restless spirits roaming around the stables."

She leaned against the wooden doorframe, studying the stall. "I always thought a stable would smell like manure."

"Some do." He shook his head. "Not mine." He put in enough hours with the horses to make sure. No matter who owned the animals, their care and well-being was a matter of pride for Andres.

Rayo pulled toward her again. "Will he bite?"

"No. He's an attention hog, though. Once he's got your number, he won't let up."

"Really…" Rayo stretched out his neck. "I wonder who you take after," she murmured, running her fingers along his jaw. The frickin' horse sighed.

A second later her words sunk in. He swung around and found her lavishing attention on the horse. Damn if jealousy wasn't taking a bite at his ass.

Her gentle laughter stopped him from calling Rayo the string of names he was about to spew. Admiration filled him as he watched her move with such confidence. Not many women could handle themselves around a spirited thoroughbred. He reached over to the shelf and pulled down an airtight container. "Here." He shook out some sugar cubes, placed them in her palm, enjoying the curiosity in her gaze. Rayo, glutton that he was, went straight for the treat. "Step forward." He cupped her elbow, murmuring instructions by her ear. "Lead him back in."

"Is he always like this?" Her dark brows rose in amusement.

"Nah. Guess he knows how to win over a pretty girl."

Her smile dimmed, then she curled perfect nails into her palm as she put some space between them. "I want to apologize—"

"Don't." She tensed up enough that Rayo stopped chewing and set his ears back. Shit. Explaining the history between him and Alex would be like taking a kick to the jewels. "Alex probably didn't realize what he said or how he said it." He tapped the brush on his thigh. "Maybe he was getting one in, but this had nothing to do with you, Doc." She cocked her head, waiting for an explanation but was too polite to ask. "We have a long history; maybe I'll tell you about it over a cold beer some day."

"I don't drink while I'm working."

He grinned at how she created the perfect out. As the town doctor, she was always on duty. "Then I guess you won't be hearing the story."

She shook her head, a steely look in her hazel eyes. Damned if he didn't like getting her riled. "Well that blows the 'nice guy' theory out of the water." She snorted. "Not exactly a shock."

"Doc. I'm a lotta things." He zeroed in on her mouth, advancing with careful steps until the subtle scent of flowers surrounded him. "Nice isn't really one of them. In fact…" His voice lowered. "If you knew what I wanted to do to you, 'nice guy' would be the furthest thing from your mind." He moved in closer, his breath fanning across her cheek. "I know it's the furthest thing from mine."

Monica held her ground, revealing another side of her personality to him. She was damn stubborn when she wanted to be. For a mad second, he wanted to back her into the corner.

Kiss her until she melted against him. Then he'd explore every curve, reach under her skirt and hear her beg him to take her against the rough boards. His cock swelled, and he swallowed hard as he fought the urge to grab her and do just that.

She bit the corner of her lip, and he groaned. The brush hit the ground, and his hands went to her slim hips.

"An—" The way her lips parted around his name made it perfect for stealing a kiss. He devoured the second syllable, licking the remnants off her bottom lip. He was still savoring the taste of her when her hands came up, pushing at his chest to create a gap between them. "I can't do this," she whispered against his lips. "I'm…"

His shoulders tensed. What was she?

"I'm your doctor. Th-this is unethical."

His breath rushed out. He grinned, happy to clear her conscience. "You're *a* doctor, Monica Vasquez. But you don't have to be *my* doctor." She could be the uptight doctor with anyone else. But he wanted the woman whose lips parted for a heartbeat. Just long enough to let him taste the sweetness of her mouth.

The pressure against his chest wavered, but she didn't quite give in. His growing erection insisted the corner was still a possibility. Better yet, he could have her on that bench, sitting astride him while those fingers ran across his chest. He could swear her full lips pulled into a soft smile.

"Hmm, forgot you prefer to self-diagnose."

Rayo sidestepped, and a faint conversation caught their attention. He set her back, scooped up the brush, placing it in her hand a few seconds before company arrived. Moving around the horse, he made a needed adjustment to his fly. Monica's delicate hand moved over Rayo with sure strokes. "You're a natural, Doc." He couldn't help but watch her. What would it be like to feel those graceful hands caressing his skin? Her slender fingers curling around his arms while she pressed herself against him? He cleared his throat, shifting his gaze to her face. "I won't be responsible if this nag flips over like a lap hound wanting his belly rubbed."

"*Doctora.*" Lupe Escobedo's short, pear-shaped frame stood at the stall door. "This"—Lupe shot him a hostile glare—"would get people talking in the most *in*appropriate manner."

David Barrios, police chief and a long-time friend, hid his smile beneath his full moustache as he stood next to Lupe.

"Of course, Lupe. I was checking on Andres and got distracted by Rayo." She returned the brush to Andres, her soft fingers barely touching his rough ones.

Barrios stepped back from the doorway, tipping his hat. "Ma'am."

"Chief," she acknowledged as she swept by them both.

"We need to go." Lupe clucked as she led Monica away. "Simon is waiting with your bag. I didn't want him carrying such a heavy burden all over the ranch, trying to find you. Chief Barrios was nice enough to escort me."

"I didn't mean to keep you waiting…" Monica apologized.

As the two women walked away, Barrios lounged against the doorframe, taking in the scene. "You trying to score points with the doctor?"

"Nah." Andres ran his fingers across the blaze on Rayo's nose, keeping his gaze averted from his friend.

"Damn. You think I'm the one she's looking back at?" The chief sucked in his gut, running his hands down the front of his dark uniform.

Andres stepped back, looking out toward the empty doorway at the far end. His fists tightened with jealousy at the thought of some other man's hands on Doc, friend or not. "That ain't funny," he growled.

Barrios chuckled behind him, pushing the one button guaranteed to get a reaction. He tipped back his hat, putting his thumbs in his pockets. "Ain't? They didn't teach proper grammar at your fancy college?"

He ignored the question, having taken too much ribbing from his brother's friend over the years. "Don't you have *chieffing* to do—somewhere else?"

Barrios's face lost all amusement. "I was sure something was going to go wrong today."

The hint of trouble in cartel territory superseded any hurt feelings. "Like what?" His gut tightened. He'd started as one of the chief's unwitting volunteers years ago, thanks to Rudy, his older brother. Andres had gotten his ass in the saddle to track down a lost kid. He knew the surrounding area better than anyone. Unfortunately, the cartel had forced the department to release the volunteers and hire another half dozen men.

"I don't know. Our residents keep us on our toes sometimes."

"Saw everyone was here in uniform."

"Better safe than sorry." Shoulders slumped, he pushed himself off the doorframe. "I better get back to *chieffing* before the night catches up with me." He held on to his hat as a powerful gust sent dust and hay down the stable ahead of him. "I have to follow up on a lead about Guerrero's missing driver."

"You found him?"

"No." Trying to find a missing cartel member would be a waste of time. Nobody would talk to the law. They had enemies with rival cartels, and sometimes within their own ranks. "But the investigation turned up an unexpected connection."

"What?" Had he found someone working with Guerrero? Or against him?

Barrios's moustache quirked, then he pulled a poker face and set his hat. "You and I will definitely have to talk. But first, I need to get some answers."

"I don't know if you understand how improper it is for you to be found alone with a man in the barn."

Moni followed Lupe out of the stable. Her nails bit into her palms as she swallowed the urge to point out in what century they were living.

Growing up with a renowned doctor for a father and a socialite mother had perks. Soledad, her childhood nanny, had drilled propriety, religion, and social etiquette into her. She knew how to keep on schedule, the patron saint for every day of the year, and she could plan a charity event for hundreds. Most importantly, she'd learned to treat people with patience and respect.

"Stable."

"What?" Lupe pursed her lips.

"The horses are kept in the stable, not the barn. I'm a doctor first, Lupe. My main priority is my patient. Wherever he happens to be." Maybe appealing to the woman's ethical side would help drive home her point. "Nobody in town would raise an eyebrow if Dr. Treviño had been the one to do a follow-up."

"Dr. Treviño has the advantage of being a man."

Blood rushed through Moni's head, parading a string of ill-mannered words across the back of her mind. She chewed on the need to set the older woman in her place, better yet, to drag her into this century. Living in Dr. Treviño's considerable shadow was stressful enough. How could she compete with someone who started practicing medicine before she was born?

Breathe. Deep, cleansing breaths. The whole reason for this outing had been to try and improve their working relationship. If she didn't bite her tongue, she'd ruin the little progress she'd made.

"Well, I'm sure I'll survive having a few eyebrows raised." She'd certainly survived all the raised eyebrows, from people she cared about, the fateful night of her engagement party. The night Valdo shattered her plans for their future. *No. I won't allow those thoughts into my head.*

With a surreptitious glance around, Lupe pulled her aside and whispered, "The Calderon family may be well regarded, but you should take care." Her lips hardly moved as she continued. "They have a long history of ruining a woman's reputation before throwing her to the wolves." The stiffness in Moni's shoulders loosened. For once, Lupe seemed to be speaking to her with something akin to concern.

While she wasn't worried about "being ruined," she wondered if Andres was one of the "deviant" Calderons Lupe referred to. He seemed a nice enough guy. For the most part, he went out of his way to keep to himself when other people were around.

She bit the inside of her lip, resisting the urge to prod Lupe for more details. Gossip wasn't her thing, and one of the few items Dr. Treviño specifically warned her about not engaging in when she came here. Especially since this little town seemed to foster the behavior. "Thank you. I'll try to be mindful in the future."

"You'll find several young men in town—from good families," Lupe rushed to add. Moni took a few steps, to get Lupe going. She didn't want the woman steering the conversation to her son. In one breath Lupe would cut her down, or whoever else stood in front of her. In the next she was trying to sell her on the idea of hooking up with her son. She'd have to find a diplomatic way to put a stop to that soon.

"Simon thinks the world of you."

And there she goes. "Thanks. He's like a brother to me, even though I haven't known you both very long." Simon was nice enough, but not exactly the type to catch her attention.

His job, keeping the books for the local general store, was two blocks down the street. He dropped off and picked up his mother every day, and even came by the office during lunch on occasion. Over the last few weeks, he'd been coming by more often. Not that he'd shown any interest in her. Thankfully.

Whatever either one of them had in mind wasn't going to happen. She'd been counting the days until Dr. Treviño was free to take over his office again. Her bags had been out, ready to be packed for months, waiting for the magic words. Nothing would keep her from jetting out of town the moment she got the call about the position in Monterrey's new ambulatory group.

L uck was on his side. After overhearing the chief talking to Andres in the stable, he'd expected the officer to seek a word with him. The party was now in full swing behind the two men as they made their way slowly through the knee-deep grass. They were well outside the glare of the lights set up for the mariachis, entertaining the crowd after the rodeo.

The dark uniform Barrios wore, along with his own clothing, would help them blend into the night. The going was slow with the chief barely able to stand, but keeping him upright was preferable to leaving a drag trail.

"Where'rewe go'n?" The words slurred together as his pace faltered, shifting his weight again.

"To the last cabin. You'll get the answers you require." Barrios nodded. A sliver of doubt crept past the adrenaline rushing through his body. Barrios allowed him to lead, trusting him, accepting a drink he'd easily dosed. This had never been part of the plan, but he had come too far to turn back. He stiffened his resolve, he would do what must be done to save what was most precious to him.

They'd reached the unused cabin sitting farthest from the main house. "Take a step. That's it. Careful."

"Is's dark."

"Yes. Take a seat while I turn on the light." He got the chief settled and waited, knowing the narcotic had disoriented him enough to lose track of time. Shortly he'd be able to sort through this mire. Perhaps he'd overreacted. The questions were unexpected. Too many. Too personal. He hadn't expected anyone to unravel his secrets.

The chief's breathing evened out.

A headache thrummed along his temples. He'd have to decide what to do with this predicament. The narcotic would wipe the memory of what happened tonight, but the information he already had would remain. Having those ties leaked could bring consequences he wouldn't be able to deal with.

No. He couldn't see another way to resolve the issue and stop any further investigation into his life and Guerrero's group. With everybody occupied, he'd have just enough time for what he had to do.

Chapter Three

D r. Treviño sat behind the sturdy oak desk. An array of diplomas and certificates formed an arch on the wall behind his leather office chair. Even with all the experience he'd gained in his practice, Monica had a growing need to question his health. It was in her nature.

She tapped her short, manicured nails on the manila folder in front of her. She couldn't put this off any longer. Twice now he'd zoned out while reviewing patient files during his regular visits.

She took a deep breath, exhaling as she produced the serene smile she used while discussing a patient's illness or concern. "You don't need me to tell you you're suffering from exhaustion." Dark circles colored the heavy bags under his eyes, his shoulders drooped, and he seemed to have thinner, grayer hair than when she arrived six months ago. "But I have to ask if exhaustion is all that's wrong?"

"Old age seems to be finally catching up with me."

"Is there something I could help you with, so you aren't tied down to Mr. Guerrero?" And maybe get her home quicker, in the process.

His gaze sharpened for a moment as he stared at her, and something she couldn't identify flashed over his face. She took a deep breath and opened her mouth to apologize for being forward, but he held up his hand while shooting a glance at the closed door.

"I appreciate your concern and, of course, as a doctor you have questions about things I cannot discuss. Pablo is no ordinary patient and the circumstances are…problematic." He leaned toward her, folding his hands together, and rested his chin on top of them. He checked the door again, then directed his gaze back to her and lowered his voice. "There are dangers here you know nothing of, and I prefer to keep it that way. I have his trust, for what that is worth. It is best in such cases to ask very few questions, my dear."

She nodded. Of course the poor man was under tremendous stress. He spent days at a time locked away, his patient a man with a volatile temper and a history of violence. Not knowing what he was treating Guerrero for, or what it was he couldn't tell her, didn't leave her much to offer in the way of advice.

Doctor Treviño absently rubbed at the top of his desk. "Any news on David?"

Moni bit the inside of her lips and shook her head. "Nothing. Nobody's seen or heard from the chief since the rodeo on Saturday."

His brows met in high peaks. "Three days." He closed his hands, trying to quell a light trembling. "That does not bode well for him."

"No, definitely not." His officers had speculated about who he'd gone home with. The event drew a lot of fans, many of them women. While everyone hoped he'd gotten lucky, they didn't seem too convinced. "I didn't recognize half the people attending."

Dr. Treviño leaned back in his chair, rubbing his index finger across his right eye. "What I did find odd was having so many unfamiliar faces in the waiting area."

She'd been shocked when Lupe arrived on Monday morning, a trail of patients following her into the building. Several new patients, some curious, some expectant. "Lupe's been in a mood since yesterday. At one point we had to review the policy to see all patients, regardless of their ability to pay for the visit."

He nodded once. "I can assist you for the next few hours."

"We're trying to get you to rest," she said in her best doctor's voice. "Last night Dora stayed until we were done. I'll see if she's willing to help us cover the front desk again today."

"Thank you for your concern, Monica. I'll try to rest my old bones." He stifled a yawn, leaning in to pat her wrist with a knowing chuckle. "I need these outings, even if all I can manage is to sit and listen to Lupe complain."

Moni brushed an imaginary speck off the thigh of her black slacks. Lupe was a handful. The woman needed Xanax more than any patient she'd ever seen.

"Dealing with Lupe can take patience," he said in a fatherly tone. His light-brown eyes, faded with age and exhaustion, held a note of sympathy. "I wouldn't have reached out to you for this assignment if I thought you weren't suited."

One sentence from Dr. Reynaldo Treviño was enough to humble her. The petty comments about Lupe trying to push past the filter in her brain would have to stop.

"We're from another generation. Not everyone your age can understand the cultural niceties we grew up with." He rolled a pen back and forth, his thoughts far away. "Had I been born in Copas, I would have happily spent my life here."

There was certainly a massive generational gap. Every night she went to bed missing home and the freedom she'd taken for granted. Everyone in Copas was critical of what they considered propriety. It was as if the last fifty years of progress in the rest of the world hadn't reached here. Isolated. That's how she felt.

He shook his head, pulling back to the present. "Keep your head up, *Doctor* Vasquez." He smiled with a professor's pride for a former pupil. "I know Lupe is doing what she thinks is best. And she cares for the patients coming through this office."

Well, she certainly knew a lot *about* the patients coming through the office. "Speaking of which, I should get back before I'm called out for slacking."

"You could never be accused of shirking your duties."

A blush that matched the coral hue of her blouse made its way up her neck. If he only knew. She opened the door to find Lupe waiting—a sour look on her round face. Monica stepped back, allowing Lupe through while turning to the doctor with a cocked eyebrow. *I told you so.*

As soon as she left the room the door shut behind her, catching her heel. *What a bitch.* She steadied herself, doing a double take when she noticed the door to the last exam room closing. Her stomach dropped. This meant a patient from Guerrero's crew needed medical attention. Was that why Lupe had been waiting on them?

Per office policy, whoever occupied the corner room had to be seen first. Not only were they more likely to have a life-threatening injury, but getting the person off the premises would make for a safer environment.

Pushing the door open, she stepped in, taking careful stock of the bare counter in a green crackled finish, clean sink, and most importantly, no signs of blood. Her heels clicked, echoing in the strained silence. The forest-green privacy curtain was drawn to cover one side of the exam area. Why the mystery? Guerrero's men walked around like they owned the place. The shadow behind the curtain seemed to be the only person in the room. Three anxious steps later, she caught sight of a muscled shoulder, short dark hair, and a familiar sun tattoo.

Andres sat on the exam table, bare-chested, his palms on the cushion, fingers hanging over the edge. She exhaled, stress draining from her neck and back, a different kind of tension taking over. One that had her thankful the lab coat covered her breasts.

"Hey, Doc." An easy smile greeted her.

Coming closer, she held his gaze, careful to keep her attention from straying past his shoulders. She'd always liked Andres, despite his involvement with the cartel. He wasn't like most people from the area. He preferred to sit on the fence of propriety, keeping one foot on the railing whenever they weren't alone. That didn't mean they'd end up in a lip lock again, regardless of the little happy dance going on inside her.

"Andres?" She jammed her hands into the coat pockets.

"I was thinking I might need a follow-up."

The walls moved in on her, making the room smaller.

Her training told her Andres was fine. Yet here he was in the exam room, half dressed and looking at her like she was a decadent piece of chocolate. And the standard clinical thoughts went right out the door, replaced by a flutter somewhere beneath her throat. *Ay Dios.* She should get rid of him. Run him out. Tell him to find another doctor.

Her mouth had a mind of its own, however. "Let me grab some gloves." She pulled her hands from her pockets and turned to the cabinet. The latex should help impede any interaction. At least that's what she'd tell herself afterward.

A strong hand caught her elbow, leading her back around to stand between his knees. "No latex," he murmured, guiding her palms to settle at his bare waist.

Warm skin singed her fingertips, intensifying the flutter. Her pinky skimmed along the top of his dark jeans and western belt. "M…my hands are cold."

He was so close…too close. She swallowed, knowing what was coming, hating herself for the thrill running through her body. But kissing Andres Calderon had made her feel like she'd been missing out on something her entire life. Something only he could give her.

"We'll have to do something to warm you up." The distance between them melted away. His lips found hers. Gentle. Searching. The air around them sizzled. Work-roughened fingers curled along the side of her face. The barest pressure of his thumb on her jaw tilted her head, allowing his tongue to sweep past the seam of her sensitized lips. Heat rose between them—from him—from her? *Step back…too close.* Defiant fingers anchored to his body of their own accord.

Her coat opened. She should stop him. This could only lead to trouble. But his hand swept up her torso unhindered, to mold her left breast with delicious pressure. The edge of the demi cup gave way, dragging across her stiff nipple. Awareness rushed through her chest and the top of her arms, leaving a tingling sensation in its wake. Her body came alive, reminding her of all the things she hadn't done in way too long. Things he'd brought to mind more and more often lately. His fingers surrounded her nipple, rolling the sensitive nub with sure, gentle strokes. A jolt ran through every vital organ, slamming against the juncture of her legs.

Monica pulled away, exhaling in a rush. "*Dios mio.*" He stilled but didn't release her. She hadn't managed to put more than an inch or two between them. For some insane reason, her extremities weren't complying with her wishes.

"Mmm, sorry, Doc." His voice rumbled by her cheek as he inched up the curve of her neck. "The closest I come to religion is missionary position."

A whimper escaped her. She trembled, drenched at her core, and wanted to climb on the table with him. The flippant remark added images to those already stuck in her head—heavy-lidded eyes, generous mouth, and broad shoulders moving above her while he thrust...

Slamming her eyes shut, she yanked her hands back from where they rested, splayed high across his thighs. How had her thumbs ended up a hair's breadth away from the bulge in his jeans? And did she really need to move them?

The halfhearted plea to God had been adopted from Soledad, more from familiarity than true belief. But maybe she should have been calling out for help from above. She'd never be able to utter those words again without recalling the image of Andres Calderon, half naked, sexy as hell, and staring at her with desire.

Unsteady, she stepped back, exhaling through open lips before drawing in the next breath. He reached for her. She shifted, pulling her arm away as the door opened. Within a split second she straightened, dragging the white coat around her like a protective cloak.

She headed toward the door, glad for the sturdy heels she'd worn today. Lupe stopped at the other side of the curtain, her shoulders stiff and a disapproving frown riding her thin lips.

"I need a patient file opened for Mr. Calderon. Run a panel on him for a baseline." Somehow, she made it past without glancing over her shoulder.

"*What* tests do you want me to run?" Lupe asked.

"All of them," she snapped. Lupe's head jerked back, her eyebrows shooting high onto her narrow forehead. Moni didn't slow down. How many years had she worked with difficult patients and overbearing family members? Yet one man had been able to shake her demeanor. Not only had she blatantly ignored the moral code she'd sworn to live by, she'd been unprofessional, given in to physical urges, and her hard-won control over her emotions had slipped.

The office was occupied, as were the exam rooms, and Dora sat up front. With limited options, she turned to the ladies' room. The closed door loomed before her. *Please be available.* The last thing she needed was someone else seeing her disheveled. Months of working to gain everyone's respect would wither in the few hours the gossip took to go from one end of town to the other.

The door gave way to welcoming darkness. She flipped the lock and turned on the light before she slumped against the tiled wall to catch her breath. He hadn't touched her last time, only fueled an unexpected longing. *Damn you, Andres Calderon.* She crossed her arms over her chest, bringing the insides of her wrists over the needy tips of her breasts.

More than once, she'd had to gently—or not so gently—let a guy down. The fact she lived alone would get tongues wagging over the most casual of outings. So she wasn't going to date while she was in town, much less tumble into bed with a man. Especially not one with some sort of connection to the local cartel—no matter how her body begged her to reconsider.

The throbbing in her body began to dissipate. *Settle down and breathe deep.* Half a dozen patients still waited for care.

Monica bent over the sink, turning the knob to let cold water flow. She cupped her hands under the stream then splashed her face until she banked the fire in her cheeks. Grabbing a few paper towels, she blotted her skin dry. The stiff paper didn't soak up the moisture quickly enough. She chased a droplet down her jaw...where he'd caressed her with his thumb.

Stop it. She tossed the napkin in the wastebasket. Back straight, coat in place, senses more or less reined in, she reached for the doorknob. With a little luck she'd be able to ignore her overly sensitive nipples leading the way.

A ndres stared at the far wall, gritting his teeth as Lupe tied a rubber strip around his bicep and ran a swab over his vein.

"You're going to feel a twinge." The needle pierced his arm with a hard sting. Damn, the woman had a heavy hand. His blood pooled into the clear container as Lupe stood there, tapping her foot. The sour look on her face made him feel like a misbehaving kid who'd been sat in the corner. He should have made his getaway when she left to grab a clipboard.

Lupe switched out the tubes, writing his name on the first one.

What stupid impulse had driven him to slip in and try to score a few minutes with Monica?

What would he do with her if he got her alone? The door to the office had opened, and he'd started pulling at his shirt like a fourteen-year-old boy. So fucking stupid.

But he could still feel her hands on his skin, taste her on his lips. She'd said her hands were cold, but she'd burned a trail down to his thighs. His dick had taken control. He'd run his hands over her, enjoying every curve and valley. Even dragged his rough fingers along her face.

"Don't make a fist," Lupe snapped. She was writing his name on another tube.

"Sorry." He opened his hand, uncovering the hard pads along his palm and fingers. How could he not run her off? He wasn't an *aristo* who could sit back and order other men to do the rough work. He was a freaking ranch hand, and she was a doctor. *What the hell was I thinking*?

Touching Dr. Monica Vasquez would be his downfall. But not touching her would be a thousand times worse.

Chapter Four

"I'll get the prescription written—" Frantic knocking stopped Monica midsentence. "Excuse me, Mrs. Ramos."

Moving to the door, she opened it and found Dora standing there, wringing her hands, her bottom lip quivering. Monica's gut clenched. "Doctor Vasquez, y-you have to... come." The dusting of freckles on her nose stood out on a face as pale as the medical scrubs she was wearing.

Monica stepped out, leaving a curious granny trying to peek around the door. "What's wrong?"

Dr. Treviño came out of a nearby exam room. His brow furrowed as he took in the assistant's distress. "Is everything all right?" Dora pressed her hands to her stomach, a glassy sheen covering her eyes. "It's the chief, Doctors. He-he's..." She struggled to swallow. "Th-they want you over at the station."

Doctor Treviño turned on his heel. Monica put a steadying hand on Dora's shoulder. "The emergency room needs to be cleared, Dora. You tell Lupe to make sure it's ready when we come back."

Monica ducked into the office and grabbed her doctor's bag before rushing to catch up to Dr. Treviño. The police station was two blocks away. Her short legs made the distance seem twice as long. The heavy pack bouncing at her back, threatening to tip her over, didn't help.

Over a dozen men, both officers and civilians, stood outside the plain-faced building, their unease reaching Monica even at this distance. One man doubled over, emptying the contents of his stomach at the edge of the sidewalk. She glanced toward Dr. Treviño, expecting the calm façade he always presented. Instead, a stiff slash of his mouth, beads of sweat on his upper lip, and a fixed stare met her gaze.

The morning's coffee churned in her stomach. What had Dora learned to leave her in such a state? Why hadn't she been able to provide more details? What were they walking into? A beat-up pickup crawled past them; the grizzled driver craned his neck to catch the scene instead of watching the road. Hopefully she wouldn't have to deal with an accident also.

Monica's heart raced, more out of concern than the two-block sprint. As expected, the group's attention centered on Dr. Treviño. "David?"

"There." One of the men pointed toward the entrance. Everyone stood back from the doorway; those standing along the sidewalk allowed him through before closing ranks. She reined in her annoyance. At her height, even with the heels, she wasn't able to see the chief.

Doctor Treviño's voice carried over the crowd. "Monica, I need you to go back to the office."

Moni put the backpack down, her hand tightening around the strap at the top. Dr. Treviño had never blatantly dismissed her as if she were in the way. She wasn't budging. "I'm here to help."

"You need to get the patients cleared out as quickly as

possible. I'll take David in by the rear entrance."

Footfalls echoed behind her. The officers murmured amongst themselves. Some hung on every word, others pretended their attention was elsewhere. Doubt pierced her irritation. If there was a chance other patients would be in danger, she had to consider them first.

"Get her out of here," he said to someone behind her.

She didn't need to glance back to know who stood there. "Come on, Doc." Andres took the backpack out of her hand, slinging the strap over his shoulder.

She did *not* need a sitter. In her haste to avoid him, she stepped back, and her heel landed on an oddly shaped rock. Her foot rolled to the outside, stretching the ligaments surrounding her right ankle with a sharp pinch. Andres and one of the uniforms steadied her. Heat erupted from her cheeks.

"Sorry, Doc, I must have caught you with the bag."

Her eyes darted to the officer. "Thank you." He nodded once before he turned his back, taking the typical wide-legged cop stance.

"You okay?"

She flexed her ankle, doing a quick evaluation with no pain or pinching. Sustaining her weight would be another matter. "I'm fine." She placed her foot on the ground, shifting forward a bit before pulling back, then trying again.

"Let's have a look." Andres squatted, running his hand over the top of her foot, around the anklebone, and up her leg. Her pulse sped up, and she had little choice but to use his shoulder to steady herself. Deft fingers eased over the ligaments on the outside and inside of her foot. "Everything seems to be okay, but I'm used to horses, not women." With that, he slid his arm across her lower back, hooked it around her hip, and grabbed her under the knees as he stood.

The yelp escaped before she could stop it. She clutched at

hard muscle, holding on for dear life. "What are you doing?"

"Getting you back to the office." He managed to swivel around without hitting anyone. Someone snickered, and she glared over his shoulder. Several men turned, some doing a double take as Andres's long stride put distance between them.

Mortified, her fingers dug in to his back while she hid her face against his collarbone. Sunshine, fabric softener, and Andres filled her senses, sending a lick of heat across her breasts. "I'm fine, Andres. You can put me down."

"Yeah, 'I'm fine' didn't do me a whole lotta good, either, *Doctor*."

She pressed her lips together. Damn. Thwarted by her own words.

People stood watching, hopefully interested in what was happening behind them. Kicking her way free would only draw more unwanted attention. She'd be better off waiting until he put her down instead of throwing a tantrum—though no one could stop her from sulking during the trip. With nowhere else to turn, she studied his profile.

Soledad kept a jar of honey on the windowsill for her lavender tea. When the sun was at the right angle, you could see yellow, gold, and a little red shining through at the center—just like Andres's irises. How could the man not fascinate her? He was just like the prince she used to fantasize would sweep her off her feet. But she knew better than anyone that princes didn't really exist.

She gave an exaggerated sigh. "You didn't have to *carry* me back to the office."

"Didn't wanna wait. You woulda taken too long to limp two whole blocks."

"I didn't feel any pain." *Well, hardly any.* "I'm sure my ankle is fine."

"Let's not take any chances." He winked at her. "As I

see it, I can either carry you in my arms or toss you over my shoulder."

Typical Neanderthal mentality. She settled back to sulk, unwilling to rise to the bait.

"As much as I'd like to have your cute little ass in the air, I'm not willing to share the view with those morons."

Maybe at this distance her glare would singe his eyebrow. The jerk grinned, without sparing her a glance. The man had some damn nerve. Never mind the thrill that raced through her when he'd swept her up against his chest. *Why him? Why now?* She didn't want the complication of a man in her life. She'd had enough of that for a lifetime.

"You're going to give yourself a headache if you keep glaring at me so hard."

She chose to ignore him. "What did your people do—"

"They're not my people." He cut her off with a cold edge he'd never used before. "I hope they burn in hell for whatever they did to my friend."

Her heart squeezed. Until Dr. Treviño got back to the office, all she could do was pray.

A muscle worked along his jaw, sending a ripple through his closely groomed beard. "They're maggots, feeding off my family's stolen land. Impossible to get rid of when you can only get to a few at a time."

Get to a few at a time?

"It's my heritage." The words bled past his lips. "That's not something I'm willing to walk away from even if it's a lost cause."

Before she could ask him what he meant, they'd arrived at the office. She shifted in his arms, more than ready to put space between them. "You can put me down now."

"Will do." He set her on the sidewalk with care, his hand riding up the slope of her back. Her throat constricted, yet he seemed oblivious to the havoc he wreaked.

She gingerly tested her ankle, rotating it slowly before putting her weight on it. Once she was able to take a few steps without limping, he nodded, satisfied she was okay. "I gotta go find the doc before he disappears on me again."

She took the bag from his shoulder before meeting his eyes. "Thank you."

The twinkle was back, along with a teasing wink.

The world shrank around her again. Her gaze cut to the triangle of skin at his open collar before she did an about-face. She walked slowly to the door, unwilling to push her luck with the ankle, but paused when his booted footsteps took off, growing quicker as he got farther away. She stole a glance over her shoulder, enjoying a view of his perfect ass. Strong arms to support him. Solid core for power. Firm, tight glutes for thrust. Sex with him would likely be incredible. She stifled a whimper before ducking inside.

"What happened?"

"Is it the chief?"

"Is someone hurt?"

The avalanche of questions descended as soon as she entered the waiting area. They'd created a scene by running through the office, and anxious faces waited for answers.

"Doctor Treviño is seeing to the matter." She put one foot in front of the other, not allowing herself to slow down. "I'm certain everything will be fine." Her voice, strong and sure, was the polar opposite of her true feelings. She went back toward her office, intent on dropping her pack.

"Is it true?" Dora asked over the thumbnail she was biting.

"We need to get the office cleared out." Moni put the bag down.

"What happened?" Lupe demanded.

"I don't know. We need to get the office cleared out. Now."

"What? Why don't you know?"

The shocked tone surprised Monica. "Dr. Treviño sent me back. We need to clear everyone out as soon as possible." Lupe knew the drill. They didn't have time for this.

"I should go help Dr. Treviño."

Dora's worried stare bounced from one to the other, her teeth still holding her thumbnail in a vise.

"He'll be here shortly." Monica turned to Exam Room A, pulling the file from the bin. "Dora, I need you to man the front door while Lupe—"

"He sent you back because you couldn't—"

The side door opened. Monica gasped while Lupe's scream filled the hallway. The file went flying as she caught the nurse's limp form before she hit the floor. Apparently Lupe's years of experience hadn't quite prepared her for everything.

Dr. Treviño stood in the doorway, a weathered fruit crate in his hands. A legion of flies buzzed around, landing on the thin, blood-soaked, wooden planks. Between the slats, a moustache, nose, and eye were visible.

The chief had been found.

A ndres held his breath as Dr. Treviño stepped into the office. He rubbed the back of his neck, looking around at the people waiting for him. Not even a cricket dared break the silence weighing heavily on the group. Andres's fists tightened to the point of pain. Barrios didn't deserve whatever those animals had done to him before ending his life.

"Chief Barrios was decapitated post mortem." The doctor's voice, surprisingly strong for his haggard appearance, boomed across the room.

"What does that mean?" One of the three remaining officers whispered to the man next to him.

Monica stood at the end of his desk, lost in thought. Lupe

cocked her head, staring at the officer until the younger man squirmed. "It means"—she spat—"they killed him before they cut off his head."

"Oh." The guy crossed his arms, slinking back a step.

Grinding his teeth, Andres glared at Lupe. How the hell had she ended up in healthcare? She had no sense of dealing with people.

"The men are nervous." Mario Villa, a twelve-year veteran of the police department, spoke up. "This is a message to us—all of us." He folded his arms, looking around to the two officers who'd followed him. "We all know the danger involved in our jobs. But this is way past the line." His gaze turned back to Dr. Treviño, pleading for understanding. "I don't know how many are going to want to risk their lives to end up like…" His lips compressed, unable to utter the chief's name.

Dr. Treviño absently rapped his knuckles on the desk. He sighed, settling into his chair. "I understand you are scared."

Andres hung on every word, his chest feeling like a hollow gourd. He'd seen the fear in their eyes when he'd gone back to get Dr. Treviño. The fact that only three of the men stuck around to hear the doctor's findings was concerning, but not completely unexpected.

"You men have families to worry about," Dr. Treviño continued. "Wives, children, parents—they're all dear to us. They're the reason we do our jobs every day."

"You're living up at the house with *them*." Claudio, the third officer, spoke up. "What are you hearing about this?"

The doctor shook his head. "I'm not privy to discussions about their…business. My conversations with my patient only go as far as his health is concerned."

"Who else could do something like this?" Claudio voiced what everyone had been thinking. Decapitation was the cartel's favorite form of intimidation. Their brutal message traveled far and wide. Fear rippled through the legal community and civilians alike. "And why go after Barrios?"

Why indeed? Andres scrutinized the three officers. None of them offered a suspect. Barrios had been after someone. After the rodeo he'd been restless, expecting something to happen. If only Barrios had mentioned what the problem was or who he'd had in his sights.

They'd been friends most of their lives, worked together on numerous occasions, but why would Barrios want to share information with him? More importantly, why didn't he share it with his uniforms? Could one of them be involved in whatever Barrios was expecting? He did a mental review on the guys. The original crew were all family men. The new guys were single when they'd started. Apparently Barrios hadn't wanted to put another family man at risk. But they were young and from the area.

If circumstances had been different, he might have signed up. But since he lived under what was now a cartel roof, he couldn't even consider law enforcement.

Mario stepped up to the desk. "I thought I'd be able to do it." He pulled the badge from his uniform, dropping it on the doctor's desk. "I'm not going to risk my life or my family. I'm done." The last two officers followed suit. With the final metallic clink, Copas lost all of its law enforcement.

Despite the lack of traffic, Monica looked both ways before crossing the street. Not a soul ventured along the sidewalks besides her and Simon. He'd walked her back from the general store, helping carry the gauze, tape, alcohol, and various supplies she'd purchased. God only knew what might happen in the coming days. Lawlessness might take over.

Monica shifted a bag to her left hand and pulled the key

out of her pocket. "Let me get that for you." Simon reached around her, taking the bag from her hand. Muffled voices filtered out from the office as they entered.

"You have a call from the ranch, Doctor. I'll transfer the line." Dora put down the receiver, her sparkling eyes darting to Simon as she swiveled out of her chair to open the door leading in from the waiting area. Moni slowed her pace, glancing back over her shoulder to find Simon's full attention on Dora.

Oblivious, Lupe turned from the filing cabinet, offering a cheek for her son's kiss while her gaze sought out Dora. "The housekeeper," she supplied without missing a beat. Simon put the bags on the desk then leaned in to greet his mother.

"Lourdes—Lourdes, wait." Dr. Treviño's exasperated voice filtered out of his office. "Who is this Susana woman?"

Lupe's eyes widened, her lips forming a perfect *O*. Brow furrowed, her questioning stare swept over the group. "Susana?" she mouthed. Dora shrugged. Moni's lips parted, but Lupe quickly shushed her, stabbing at the air as she pushed away from the desk and her son, craning her neck toward the hallway.

Intrigued, Moni set the bags down to watch the scene unfold. "I see," Dr. Treviño continued in a calmer manner. "We'll be there momentarily." The muted click of the receiver settling into the cradle echoed in the quiet office.

Lupe straightened, trying to roll her office chair back to the desk with her tiptoes. Only the tension in the air kept Moni from laughing at the comical scene.

"Lupe," Dr. Treviño called from his doorway.

"Yes, Doctor?" Lupe pasted a pleasant smile on her face as she launched herself out of the chair with an audible squeak.

"Please send for Andres. We need to return to the ranch immediately."

"Yes, Doctor. Simon just came by. I'll have him go."

Simon took his cue, heading for the front door.

"When Dr. Vasquez returns ha—"

Moni pushed off from the desk. "I'm here." She followed him as he retreated back into his office. "Good." He paused. "I'm…I need to return to the ranch."

"Of course." Moni watched him shove papers into his bag with uncharacteristic disregard. "Is everything all right?"

Snapping the bag shut, he stepped out of his office and looked at her with something akin to resignation. "Yes." He drew in a deep breath. "I'll be in touch. I'm sure you'll be brought up to date on the situation." His gaze jumped to Lupe, then back. "For now, adios. I'm a phone call away if you need me." He stood up straight and squared his shoulders, walking down the hall without a backward glance. "I'll be waiting by the truck."

"Of all the—" Lupe stood close to Dora, her shoulders thrown back as she spoke in a low, fierce tone, disapproval evident in the downward tilt of her mouth.

"What was that all about?" Monica asked, after the door latched shut.

"Susana *Rueda*," Lupe hissed. "The nerve of the woman. Showing up like nothing happened, scandalizing the housekeeper."

What had she missed? Who was Susana Rueda? What did Dr. Treviño have to do with this woman?

"Poor thing," Dora chimed in.

Lupe scoffed. "I bet she didn't go to her parents because her father wouldn't have her." Dora bit her thumbnail as she nodded her agreement.

"So who is Susana Rueda?" Moni asked, close to exasperation.

"She's Andres's…um…f-friend?" Dora shrugged.

"Friend?" Lupe spat. She crossed her arms, her mouth a

slash of disapproval.

"Well, that was before," Dora clarified.

"She's still a strumpet," Lupe added in dismissal.

Monica's lips parted as she stared at Lupe. "I'm sorry, what did you say?"

Lupe shrugged. "Everyone knows about her. She disgraced her family running off the way she did with Andres."

"I see." Monica blinked. Her voice sounded strained, and she cleared her throat to cover the slip. Is this what Lupe meant when she'd warned her about the Calderons? And why did she even care? She knew she wasn't the first to notice Andres or his delectable body.

Lupe glanced at her and frowned. "What is wrong with you?"

Some small sense of self-preservation took over. She had no intention of providing a new twist to the gossip mill. Mustering as much ice as she could, she leveled a stare at Lupe and used the one name she knew would make the woman back off.

"Dr. Treviño doesn't approve of gossip, and I have no intention of breaking his rules." Before Lupe could retort, Monica turned to Dora. "Please make sure the supplies in the pack are cataloged and placed in inventory. Let me know if any patients come in."

She turned and made for the sanctuary of her office. Closing the door behind her, she sat at her desk and drew in a breath. She held her hands out, watching her fingers tremble. Ugh. Leaning back in her chair she crossed her arms, tucking the offending digits out of sight.

She was a grown woman, for crying out loud. What was wrong with her? Thank God she'd had enough of her wits about her to come up with that lie.

Fine, a few hours ago she'd been in the exam room, wrapped in Andres's arms. He'd kissed her with abandon, making her feel as if she were the most important thing in his world, making her *want* to be the most important thing in his world.

She turned in the chair, fixing her gaze out the window as her toe tapped lightly on the wooden floor. So he hadn't been forthcoming about a past female "friend" as Dora had so delicately put it. A newly arrived past female friend.

She didn't think he'd been celibate all his life, waiting for her to show up. She certainly hadn't. And she had no intention of talking about her failed engagement or her cheating ex-fiancé. Valdo's face flashed across her mind, and humiliation shot through her. Neither of them had shared anything deep about themselves.

Still, what brought the woman, this Susana, back to Copas? And back into Andres's life?

Monica took a deep breath. Andres didn't kiss her as if another woman was on his mind, but she'd already learned her lesson all too well about how fickle a man could be.

What does it matter, Monica, you're leaving soon, remember?

Could she enjoy his company without the entanglements of feelings? She hadn't planned on getting involved with anyone here. It was for the best. She would stick with her plans, stay focused on her goal, and put this dusty, throwback-to-the-middle-ages town behind her soon enough, and any thoughts of Andres along with it.

Chapter Five

A woman's laughter reached across the blanket of darkness. *Her*. The man swallowed the word with bitterness. Splashing. Too much for one person. She would be surrounded by her men.

The din led him downriver to the edge of the clearing by the men's swimming hole. Three bodies engaged in a sordid dance. *Slut*. She was nude; a bald man fondled her breasts. A second man, his shoulders darkened with ink, swatted at her bare bottom as she slipped and slid out of the river.

"Lalo, come on." Her breath escaped in a rush. "You're missing all the fun."

Whore. What else would one call a woman who compromised herself with three—*three*—men? He'd had such high hopes for Pablo Guerrero's heir. She'd come to live with her father years ago. A young, innocent girl ripe with promise for the future.

"He's got to keep his damn eyes open, baby." Both men followed her out of the water. Their bodies were heavy with arousal, yet none showed a sliver of embarrassment over their nudity. "And they sure as hell shouldn't be following your pussy around."

She lay on the clothes scattered along the bank and opened her legs wide.

No. A scream curdled in his throat, but he managed to hold his tongue. How could she violate a place where the family had spent so many joyous hours playing with their children?

Her hips rolled back while her hand ran over her breast and belly to burrow through the curls on her mound. The tall one stared down at her offering. "I thought you liked my pussy," she pouted.

A tattooed arm reached down between his legs, his hand curling around the jutting root. "Doesn't this tell you how much I like your pussy?"

She crumbled first, coming up on her elbow. "I want it. But I can't decide where." Her giggle rent the silence while her hand continued working between her legs.

"How about you come take care of what you started." He flexed his hips. "Then we can see how you'll finish."

She pushed up on her knees in one fluid motion, swatting away a garment stuck to her back. One finger curled, calling him closer.

The man's self-assured smile mocked him from afar. Paloma's dainty hand fondled his sack then ran along his length. "If you make me come like the other day, I'll let you fuck me any way you want."

His teeth glinted in the moonlight. "Here. Take it." His hands went into her hair. She drew him in, her lips closing around him in a greedy gesture. "You're gonna let me finish this time. *Mmmm.*"

His lip curled in disgust at the obscenities she allowed. The wickedness of her act taunted him. He didn't want to watch—he closed his eyes against the sight. Moans, sucking, and the other men's encouragement echoed in his ears, planting images in his mind, shooting his lids open.

Paloma certainly wasn't the woman he thought she was. How could she allow such things?

"Fuck, that's hot!" The voice came from farther in the shadows. Their sentry. His attention clearly centered on the spectacle before him instead of on their surroundings.

She collapsed, her breathing harsh. Her hands were at her breasts, fondling herself while the man fell to his knees before her. "You liked?"

Both men answered.

Her laughter rang out. The vicious sound scratched down his spine.

"No." She pushed at a tattooed shoulder. "Flip over. I want you on your back, like the other day." The ape followed her instructions. "This way Capo can get a little something, too." Her coy suggestion had the fool trying to kick free of his pants to get to her.

The whore settled across his shoulders. Her hand went between her legs. "Oh yeah." She hissed. "You worry about blowing my mind, lover. I'll take care of blowing Capo." Pulling her hair back, she reached out. "Bring your bad-boy self over here."

He'd had such plans for her. Wife. Mother. A woman who could continue the family line in a place stolen from under them. She'd shattered the image he'd had and the plans he'd spent years cultivating. In one vile stroke, she'd ruined *everything*.

Led on by a dark hatred, he crept through the scrub brush, taking advantage of the noise raised by the whore and her men. Coming up behind the sentry was easy. The lust-blinded fool was on his knees, pleasuring himself while watching the others. Inch by inch he pulled out the sharp blade he kept as his constant companion. A single step brought him directly behind the man; a quick grab of the head to pull it back exposed the neck. The sacrifice never made a sound as the blade ensured he never would again. Dropping the body and the knife to the sand, he slid the gun from the dead man's holster and took aim.

Fate offered up an unexpected opportunity to right a long overdue wrong.

Chapter Six

Andres squinted into the distance. Three vultures circled the trees, diving for a few seconds before returning to hold the pattern. Likely some animal had become dinner for the scavengers. The sight became more common as the summer days grew hotter.

Right now he felt much like carrion himself. Susana's reappearance had blindsided him. *What was she doing here?* Obviously things hadn't worked out with her baby's father, and her father had probably shut the door in her face. But after everything, why would she show up at the ranch?

He'd been dumbfounded on the drive home. While he'd been trying to wrap his head around the news, Dr. Treviño had gone on about family and support. What about how she'd destroyed his relationship with his family and his friendship with Alex? He'd thought it couldn't get worse, then he'd learned Susana and the baby would be staying in the main house. What was now Guerrero's home.

Bile churned in his stomach at the memories. He buckled down, letting Bailarina set the pace on their return to the stable. Her hot pink mane danced in the wind. Paloma had an upscale stylist come in to do the dye job on a regular basis. News of the chief's disappearance had spread within hours, so the prissy little douche had called to say he wouldn't make the trip. As Bailarina's groom, he'd have to take her up to Monterrey in a trailer the next time her mane and tail needed a touch-up.

He loved horses, regardless of breed or, in this case, fashion statement. He'd been able to talk Paloma into dying the mane instead of the entire horse. He hated to admit it, but the contrast in the thoroughbred's rare white coat and the hot pink actually looked good. Though how the horse ended up named for a ballerina was still beyond him.

She slowed to a trot, wanting to enter the stable like a lady. Despite his thoughts, he smiled and patted her neck. No matter the species, a female was still a female.

Alex caught them at the door. "Where the hell've you been?"

The two ranch hands stacking hay ducked their heads and kept working. Much as he wanted to work things out with Alex, as usual, now was not the time. "I took Bailarina out to stretch her legs." The wind picked up, whipping the words from his lips.

Alex glared at him. "Treviño is asking for you. Go find Manny, then get your asses up the hill."

Andres didn't appreciate having orders barked at him. He opened his mouth to utter a comeback when a baby's wail cut the tension between them. Alex had probably been caught off guard, too. His angry retort died on his lips. He wondered what was up, but instead of asking Alex and making things worse, he rode Bailarina over to the bunkhouse.

Dismounting, he tossed the reins around the corner support in one fluid motion. "I'll be right back, girl." He made no effort to silence his footfalls on the uneven boards, the boots announcing his arrival at the long, shotgun-style cabin. Experience told him to make his presence known, or the guys might think someone was sneaking in. More than one ranch hand had gotten a gun pointed at him for trying to be considerate to those sleeping.

Several men looked up from their card game. A few men lay in bed, reading or catching up on sleep. One dismissed him, another pulled his weapon from under the pillow. Manuel, one of the night guards, returned his stare from the back corner. "Treviño wants you up at the house." He turned and walked out, not waiting to see if Manuel followed or not. They already considered him an errand boy; no use giving anyone an opportunity to send him back with a damn message.

The screen door slammed shut. Manuel's head popped out the collar of a T-shirt while Andres mounted. He ran a hand through his dark hair, trying to settle the rumpled cluster. "What's he want?"

"No idea, man." He pulled on the reins, keeping her from heading back to her stall. "Alex sent me to get you so we could both head over to the house."

Manuel yawned, rubbing his eyes as he followed on foot.

Bailarina left the grassy area behind, then pulled up to the house before Manuel had even made it to the clearing. Alex stood out back trading words with Dr. Treviño. The old man looked tired enough to drop at any second. Barrios's murder must be weighing on him.

"How does it matter who went to ge—"

"Andres." Dr. Treviño left Alex midsentence. "I'm glad you joined us." Andres dismounted, holding the reins behind him in a tight grip. "Pablo is concerned, my boy. Paloma didn't come down for brunch this morning."

Andres frowned. Why would he be called about Paloma?

"When the housekeeper went to check on her she found the room empty. Her car is here, so are her personal belongings, but she and her men are missing. Nobody remembers seeing her after dinner last night."

Andres stiffened. "Shit." A sick feeling rolled through his stomach.

"Pablo wants to question the sentry on duty last night." He nodded toward Manuel, still on the far side of the quarter-mile clearing. "He was watching the back of the house. Maybe he has some information he can provide to figure out where the girl is."

Pablo Guerrero asking to talk to you wasn't a good omen. Likely why Dr. Treviño had been the one to send for them.

Bailarina's nose bumped his back. He should get on the horse and go. If Paloma was drunk or high or shacked up with one of the guys, Guerrero would be furious. Regardless of her age, she was still his little girl. Whoever she'd taken off with was going to wish he were dead.

Dead...birds... A growing realization sent his blood pumping until his ears buzzed. "Let me..." He cut off his words and jammed his foot into the stirrup instead. Better to be sure before starting a panic. "Let me check on something."

"Get back here, *pendejo*," Alex hollered.

"Let the boy..."

Dr. Treviño's words faded as he rode around the house, pulling wide to avoid the propane tank behind the kitchen. "Go on, girl." Bailarina's hoofs thundered against the packed earth. He searched the sky. Vultures. The scavengers could find an animal within hours of death. *Please...* He rode on, nearing the old swimming hole.

A coyote scrambled out of the trees, a bundle firmly grasped between his teeth. Andres pulled back, bringing the horse to a hard stop. A second, larger coyote, jumped out after the runt. They growled, teeth bared, mouths and coats bloody. The runt held his ground. They tumbled over each other in combat, but Andres became oblivious. His eyes were drawn to the thumb and two fingers remaining on the hand the animal had dropped.

Bailarina circled, adding to his urge to heave up his measly dinner. "Shhh," he soothed, straining to see into the wooded area. "They're too busy to bother with us." A man's shoe lay in the distance. Blood covered the rocks by the river. He couldn't get close, not with the animals taking over the area. Better to have someone come with a weapon and scatter the wildlife.

A dire sense of foreboding intensified as he maneuvered Bailarina around and rode back to the ranch. "Sorry, girl. We're almost done." Hopefully the words wouldn't be prophetic.

Guerrero's thick voice reached him from around the corner. "...to tell anyone when she didn't come back?" His blunt, deeply grooved features reddened as he pounded his beefy fists into his victim while the others watched. Manuel was on his knees, his face a bloody mess.

Why wasn't anyone stopping the beating?

Tension engulfed him, adding to the horse's skittishness. The run, blood, death, and wild animals. Now this. How could he expect her to be calm?

Dr. Treviño stood away from the thrashing. He waved Andres back while he scurried over.

Another thud, flesh on flesh, followed by a scream. Andres pulled his foot out of the stirrup. If they weren't going to do something...

"No." Dr. Treviño grabbed him by the wrist. Sunken eyes bore into his with a wordless plea. He glanced at Guerrero, wearing slacks and a dress shirt while using his arm like a battering ram. "Quickly. What did you find?"

"The swimming hole downstream..." How could he explain the carnage he expected them to find? "I couldn't get a good look, but there's blood and at least one body."

Dr. Treviño stared at him, his brow unfurling. He worked

to swallow. The old man had his sympathy. While the doctor had likely seen a multitude of bodies before, the savage way he'd find this one, or ones, was unimaginable. If Paloma's body was among those slaughtered, he'd have to tell Guerrero.

"Go on." Dr. Treviño waved, motioning toward the stable. "Get out…get out of here." His brusque tone broke with his words. "He doesn't need to see her horse right now."

"Have them take a gun." Stupid thing to say. After so many years he still wasn't used to being around people who were armed at all times. "Scavengers—" His stomach rolled. "Scavengers got to 'em already."

The doctor nodded.

"Ask the doctor." Manuel's voice warbled over the damage to his mouth. "L-l-last night… Hhhe—"

"Her body is by the river, Pablo," Dr. Treviño announced.

Andres whipped back to stare over his shoulder, wide-eyed. *What was he doing? Trying to get himself killed? They didn't even know if Paloma was down there yet.* Whether she was or not, he hadn't expected the doctor's blunt notification.

"*Noooooo.*" Guerrero's anguished cry tore from his throat. Eyes wide, the wounded bull glared down to where Manuel scrambled in the dirt.

Andres turned away, urging Bailarina on. Bile bubbled up his esophagus. His brain couldn't process what was happening.

"The doct—" Gunfire cut off the desperate words. One bullet after another echoed behind him. This time he let the thoroughbred set the pace.

Andres followed Dr. Treviño and Monica into the office. What was he doing here? After what he went through yesterday, he wasn't sure he ever wanted to be included in anything Dr. Treviño shared again. He hadn't slept much.

Every time he closed his eyes the image of what happened replayed in his mind. Manuel hadn't been an angel, but he didn't deserve to die while pleading for the doctor's help.

Monica made herself comfortable in the high-backed office chair. He went around her, letting himself drop into the seat with the weight he'd been carrying for the last eighteen hours. Fear. Remorse. Guilt.

Monica snuck a glance at him. He sat up, conscious of the fact he was supposed to act normal.

Dr. Treviño took a seat, scooting in to lean forward on his desk. "Monica, have any of Pablo Guerrero's men come to the office?"

"One was here a few days ago." She glanced in his direction before her gaze returned to the doctor. "Why?"

"But no one has been here since yesterday?" Dr. Treviño prodded.

"No." She shook her head. "Is something wrong?"

Dr. Treviño's eyes bored into his. Did he want her to hear details about the atrocity by the swimming hole? His shoulders pressed into the chair back. Maybe both doctors were used to seeing people dead, but he never wanted to see another body part being dragged around by wild animals again.

"What happened?" she persisted.

Andres swallowed hard. His hands curled into fists.

Dr. Treviño stared down at the desk for a moment. He took a deep breath before addressing Monica. "What I'm about to tell you cannot leave this room. Do you understand?"

"Yes." She sat straighter, crossing her ankles in the process.

"Not even to the staff."

She nodded, adjusting her doctor's coat around the yellow embroidery on the front of her blouse.

"Pablo Guerrero's daughter was killed. Andres found the bodies yesterday."

Her hands shot to her chest. She turned, her eyes sad and compassionate. "Are you okay?" He forced himself to nod, because they expected an answer, though he might never be okay again.

"We had other repercussions to deal with."

The shots ricocheted in his memory.

"Alex took it upon himself to hand off to Andres the duties I asked him to perform." Dr. Treviño shook his head. "He should never have done so."

The unexpected confession lifted a weight off his being, leaving him lightheaded. He wasn't supposed to have been the one to call Manuel—not that he wished it on Alex. But Manuel knew the risks. Cartel members traded their lives on a daily basis for a hefty paycheck.

His remorse stemmed from calling Manuel to his ultimate death. Hearing the task shouldn't have been his to begin with gave him a sliver of peace.

"Wait, bodies?" Monica looked from one to another. "How many?"

"Two of her bodyguards were killed along with her." Dr. Treviño continued. "The third is missing and believed to be the killer."

Money was thrown around with no regard, and lives were expendable. But he still found it hard to imagine Damian killing Paloma. He actually thought there was something more between them. Then there were the times he'd covered for Andres, distracting Paloma or diffusing situations before they got out of hand. Andres wondered if his body would be found down the river, another victim.

"I wanted to confirm he hadn't shown up here for whatever reason."

"No, and the girls haven't mentioned anyone coming in while I was with patients." Moni worried the corner of her mouth. "Why the secrecy about what happened?"

Dr. Treviño's brow furrowed. "I don't know if Pablo is in denial or if he doesn't want to appear weak. He has a huge amount of money tied up in and around Copas." He tapped his fingers on the desk absentmindedly. "Uprooting his organization would be a costly task. Not something he'd do unless he was in dire straits."

Andres's heart sank. The chances of getting his family's holding back were next to nothing.

Dr. Treviño snapped to attention. "Dora closed the office since all the morning appointments are done. Why don't you two go out and get a bite to eat? I'm due to talk with Lupe next. I'll see if she has news on anyone showing up unexpectedly."

Monica got up, and he followed suit. He reached around her for the doorknob, his hand still unsteady. Their fingers collided, and she pulled away, shooting him a confused look. *Damn calluses.* His grip on the knob tightened.

"You're frozen."

He shrugged. Over her head he saw Lupe swiveling around in her chair, pretending not to hang on every word. Truth be told, he hadn't been able to get warm since he'd ridden into the stable yesterday. Rey had been going full force, tossing buckets and sending hay flying all over the place. He'd spent hours trying to settle the horses. With the threat of a killer lurking in the area the poor animals hadn't been let out to pasture.

Lupe passed by them without sparing a glance. The door clicked closed behind her.

"How about we grab a cup of coffee to help warm you up first?" Monica headed to the coffee station. "We can go to the café when they're done." She offered him a small smile then stretched on her tiptoes to get cups out of the cabinet. "I'm sure Lupe would have a fit if we left them here alone with the doors locked."

He reached past her, their hands colliding again when

she tried to move out of the way. He pulled back, trying to keep his fingers from folding of their own accord. *Shit*. Sure enough, when he brought the cups level, she was looking at him with concern. "Sorry, Doc," he mumbled. "My hands are rough." He put the mugs on the counter and pulled back.

She cocked her head, sending her long hair sliding over her shoulder. "You work hard, Andres. There's no shame in that." Then to his horror, she took his hand in hers. He stiffened, and it took everything inside him not to yank his hand away.

"Do they hurt?" She ran her fingers along the palm in a touch that could easily become a caress.

"No." He was well past hurting, the layers toughening with the chores.

"Would you like me to get you something to help?"

Would getting rid of the calluses make any difference? "Not if that makes you my doctor."

She gave him that cock-hardening glare, then her lips twitched. "I'm already your doctor." She released his hand. "I have a file and everything."

Andres managed a weak smile.

She rinsed the mugs then wiped down the sink. He took the "Doctors keep you in stitches" mug she offered and fixed his coffee while she flicked a pink envelope back and forth. "You like coffee with your cream, too?" she teased. The mountain of creamer she added was almost as big as the one in his cup.

She poured the coffee then sipped from her mug. "Get any sleep last night?"

He wrapped his fingers around the column of *X*s on the handle. "Not a whole lot."

"Do you need something to help you rest?" She studied him, digging into him like she'd never done before.

He shook his head and shifted his weight from one foot to

the other. *What did she see when she looked at him like that? Fear? Guilt?* She didn't have to tell him he looked like hell. "I'm all right."

"You know, I got your test results back. They were *very* boring. Nothing at all wrong with you."

He looked at her over the cup rim. He'd forgotten about going along with her request for a blood test.

"And Lupe was certainly thorough." Doc took a deep breath. "She literally ran *every* test."

Yeah, the woman had nearly drained his left arm. She might have kept going if not for Dora interrupting.

"You'll be glad to hear you *aren't* pregnant."

He choked, sending a knot of scalding coffee down his throat, making his eyes water. The nurse was a real piece of work. "Tha—that's good news."

Monica cocked her head. Her black hair cascaded over her shoulder. "Now I know something's wrong."

"What? Why?"

"Any other time you would have said 'Don't worry Doc, the baby's not yours.'"

His smile faltered. No, he'd never utter those words. Not when he'd been on the receiving end of the statement once before.

Deep inside he'd known. They'd gone to the States together—his grand plan to save Susana from all the cartel bullshit. Unfortunately, with the U.S. struggling through an economic crisis, things had started out bad and only got worse. When she'd given him the news she was pregnant, he'd been dumbfounded. He'd insisted they go home. That's when she'd clarified the situation—without a doubt—then left to be with her baby's father. His fingers grew cold again. He wrapped them around the mug, letting the heat filter through his skin. Doc's brows drew together over her hazel eyes.

She couldn't have known—nobody did. But still, the

words hit him right in the chest. Especially because they'd come from her. He didn't want her concerned. He didn't want her to ask questions, to find out about that part of his life. How he'd failed everyone. His family. Susana. Himself. Why he wasn't good enough for her.

The baby's not yours…

"We could change that, you know. The exam room's open, and the front door's locked. I bet we wouldn't notice if the cushion isn't too comfortable."

The concern evaporated, replaced by her deadly stare.

He smiled behind his mug. Yeah, he'd be all right.

Chapter Seven

Monica studied her thumbnail. She scraped away a sliver of polish smeared around the edge of her cuticle. This creation would be Blueberry Burst. A combination of midnight blue layered with Blueberry Surprise and tipped with glitter. The perfect match for tomorrow's outfit. Too bad the polish had to come off.

Beauty treatments, hair conditioners, and nail art had never been of any great interest to her. But when a girl was stuck in a tiny apartment over her office and had absolutely *nothing* to do with her nights, she got creative. Over the past few weeks her nail kit doubled in size as she practiced her new hobby. She'd done well. Even the swirls and layered designs turned out better than expected. Unfortunately, all the glitzy colors came off before bedtime.

She settled back on the sofa, trying to stay away the rough material. It was clearly made for sitting, not relaxing. The cushions were tolerable thanks to the lavender cashmere throw her sister-in-law, Tessa, gave her last Christmas.

She'd have to drive out toward the interstate and see if she could get a signal. Weeks had gone by without hearing from Kris and Tessa. She missed the long talks they shared over pizza and beer. Tessa had settled into married life well while Kris, her adopted brother, was still working on a few rough edges. Masquerading as cartel for ten years could really mess with a person. But the assignment had uncovered the man who'd killed his parents, her aunt and uncle, in the crossfire of a cartel shootout.

As if on cue, the satellite phone she kept hidden beeped from the vicinity of her bedroom. She tossed the throw and shot off the couch, banging her shin on the coffee table. By some miracle, she managed to catch the container with nail polish remover she used to soak her brushes.

Limping, she reached her backpack and yanked the zipper around the side pocket.

"Hello." Her voice sounded both anxious and breathless.

"I need you." Kris's voice came across strong and commanding.

Her grin faded. They were the same words she'd uttered when she'd been praying for news that Tessa wasn't dead in the raid that had netted Kris a major drug kingpin back in Monterrey. "*Dios mio.*"

Where the heck had Kris sent her? Monica pulled into a cluster of trees surrounding an odd rock formation at the foot of the Sierra Madre. Maneuvering through the country roads had been a long, arduous process. The area was uneven, with narrow, winding sections she couldn't always see clearly without using the headlights. Her poor little car had bottomed out on several cavernous potholes.

She peered into the murky darkness wishing for a few seconds of moonlight. Was she alone? Was someone out there watching her? And where exactly was she? If this was Rancho del Sol's fence line, the property was larger than she thought, and twice as dangerous. After what happened, Guerrero might have guards posted.

Kris's contact arranged for someone to lead her to him for medical care. But he hadn't offered a clue as to whom she was meeting. Only the assurance she'd be safe and her guide could be trusted.

This task left no room for fear. Kris wouldn't put her in danger. He wouldn't have asked her for help if it wasn't absolutely necessary.

Minutes crawled by. She dragged her moist palms over her thighs. She'd have to remember to refer to Kris as Angel, his code name. And she'd just gotten used to calling him Kris again.

Where was this guy? So far, only the crickets serenading her had made their presence known. She was early, but she should be able to see, or at least hear, a vehicle coming. Then again, she didn't exactly know where to look. If he had four-wheel drive, he could come from anywhere, even the mountain range extending to her left. Unnerved, she peered around, this time in every direction.

In the distance, a rider approached on horseback. Her heartbeat hammered in her throat. *Angel-Angel-Angel.* She pulled the backpack over then checked the switch on the dome light. Off, same as when she left the house. *No fear.* After a few deep, cleansing breaths, she stepped out of the car. While she wouldn't turn tail and run, the urge to do so mushroomed within her.

How could Kris do this every day? He'd lived in the heart of danger for years and thrived.

Rayo's markings came into view before she could fully make out the rider. So, someone from the ranch. Should she be grateful or worried?

Our Father who art in heaven...

Andres dismounted. His clothes, as dark as hers, blended in with the surroundings. Mad laughter bubbled in her chest. Why would a man insist on wearing a hat if the sun wasn't shining overhead?

He reached the fence, pulling Rayo behind him. "What are you doing here?" The low rumble didn't hide his annoyance.

She froze. Was this a test? Was he her contact or did they meet by coincidence? What would bring him out at this hour?

"Do you have any idea what you're getting yourself into?" He rubbed the muscles at the back of his neck. Rayo sidestepped, flattening his ears.

"Yes." She straightened her spine, answering with more bravado than she felt. "I'm aware of the potential danger."

"Keep your voice down." He cursed under his breath. The truth of his question slapped her in the face. Did she know what she was doing? And with whom? According to Kris's contact, the man who would guide her could be trusted. So who was he really working for? And what would happen once he took her to the patient?

Rayo pawed at the ground, anxious to get going.

"All I know is someone needs medical attention. I'm it. Regardless of what side of the law the patient is on."

His breath whooshed out, and he shook his head. "So you didn't know who you were coming to meet, either?" She shook her head. "How the hell—?" He raked a hand over his beard. "All right." His shoulders settled, and he cleared his expression. "Let's just get you up so we can go."

The backpack slid down to her elbow. She braced herself, letting the momentum swing her arm, bringing the bag high enough over the fence for him to pluck out of her hands. Flipping the strap over his shoulder, he stepped back, waiting for her to come over. She climbed the rustic rail fence like a ladder, swinging her leg over the top with the enthusiasm of a ten-year-old. Her hips swiveled, and a light breeze licked at a bare strip along the base of her spine. Strong hands caught her waist and helped her climb down. Her boots hit solid ground, but his hands lingered along her hips. She turned and tilted her head back, farther than usual, to find his darkened features. "Damn, Doc, where's the rest of you?"

She sent him a thin-lipped glare while tucking in the back of her shirt. "I couldn't exactly wear heels to traipse around the brush, now could I?"

He crowded her, sending her backpedaling until the fence hit her shoulder blades, then planted his hands along the top rail on either side of her. She leaned away, reaching out at her sides for some much-needed support. Apprehension tightened her belly. Even in the darkness, the intensity in his eyes scattered her thoughts in a dozen directions. What was he playing at? Testing scare tactics to see what worked best? Because so far, he'd scored a ten.

"Let's get something straight."

She flinched at his harsh whisper.

"If we're going to pull this off, you need to get past this 'offended miss' thing you have going."

Unlike her, this obviously wasn't the first time Andres went sneaking around in the dark. He had to know where his people were, and what they'd be looking out for...right? She bit back the retort and gave an answering nod. Some of the tension left his body, but his arms still bracketed her. "H-how..." The throaty timbre of her voice caught her off guard. "Are we supposed to play this?"

His gaze made a slow sweep down her face. "There aren't many reasons you'd be meeting me in the middle of the night."

Memories of the morning at the clinic flooded her mind's eye, drawing her nipples into tight buds. *Dios*. How was she supposed to keep it together when they were all alone, and she knew how her body reacted to him?

"Okay." Where did that breathless note come from? Was it that he'd taken over her personal space? Apprehension over what was to come? Or anticipation of it?

"You don't exactly fit the part."

Her breath caught and something akin to humiliation pulled at her insides. She fought to keep herself from shrinking back. What could she possibly say? This must be some record. Usually a guy waited until after they'd slept together to decide he'd pass on her after all.

"You're buttoned up to your neck, your hair's pulled back and braided, and you're practically running away from me. None of that reads 'come get me.'"

She blinked in rapid succession, the sense of inferiority fading away. His words started to sink in. Of course, she must look closer to a Sunday school teacher than a woman out to meet her lover. *Lover*. Dear Lord. A sliver of much-needed confidence seeped back into her. She bit the corner of her bottom lip, trying to form a response. Scattered thoughts tangled the words she tried to string together. She could do this, play this part, for Kris. Unclenching the rail, she reached for her braid and pulled the dark elastic from the bottom.

He caught her hand, his rough fingers circling her wrist as he lowered it. His gaze on hers, he slowly worked his fingers into her hair, loosening the tight plaits.

Wetness dampened the juncture between her thighs, and she curled her fingers around the fence for support.

His attention dropped to her left breast, where her hair unfurled link by link. A ragged breath echoed between them. His?

His gaze zeroed in on her mouth, and the wood creaked behind her. "Do that thing to your lip." The words were barely a rumble beneath his breath.

"What?"

Keeping his left hand in her hair, he cupped the back of

her head, tilting her up, and her lips parted with the rush of her breath. Her heart thundered at the sight of him. The dark intensity in his eyes changed, focusing on her as a woman instead of someone who'd pushed one too many buttons.

His mouth came down on hers, demanding entry and the freedom to explore at will. She should push at him, object at the way he handled her, or at least offer some token protest. Instead she whimpered, opening to him, letting him take his fill, and enjoying every wondrous stroke of his tongue against hers.

He pressed his body closer, and moisture pooled at her core. Long fingers splayed at her back, slipping down to the base of her spine. He drew her forward until her breasts flattened against him and every hard inch of his length pressed into her belly. Her fingers dug into the tight muscles of his arm and back, cursing the layers of clothing keeping her at bay.

A thrill shot through her as his teeth scraped the edge of her lip, nipping at her, then his tongue came back to lave the spot before he pulled back. She followed, much to his apparent satisfaction. "Better," he said with half-lidded eyes.

He was too arrogant for his own good. And she was way too happy with him kissing her, sending delicious shivers down her body with every touch. Shaking off the haze of desire, she lowered her hands. His gaze shot left, like he hadn't expected her to release him.

"One more thing," he whispered at her temple. His fingers came to her throat, fussing with the top button on her blouse then moving on to the next. An array of goose bumps fanned over her chest from the spot his knuckles brushed. Damn him. She didn't know who she hated more right now. Him or her traitorous body.

The inside of his wrist settled against her left breast, teasing the stiff peak with not nearly enough pressure. Deft fingers continued slipping buttons open to expose her heated skin as her pulse thrummed in her ears. She looked down, biting her lip as her breasts rose with each breath. How far was he planning to go? *How far will I let him go?* Finally, he reached the button holding her blouse closed level with the base of her bra.

Several cocktail dresses with plunging necklines hung in her closet back home, yet she'd never been more exposed than she was right now. He took in his handiwork, and his lips pulled into that sexy half smile of his.

The back of his index finger slid along her chest and over the swell of her cleavage before stopping to retrace the last few inches. "Now, isn't this better?"

"I think we would have been able to pull it off either way." Her voice belied the riot of emotions she grappled with.

He dropped his hands to her hips, setting her back a few inches. She clenched her thighs, refusing to protest the loss, telling herself she was thankful for the distance. "Is that so?"

She nodded.

"You think someone would believe you'd come out here in the middle of the night and wouldn't end up naked under me?"

She swallowed a squeak. "Easy enough. I'd tell them you'd pissed me off." She quirked a brow. "Anyone who knows you would believe my explanation."

He had the audacity to grin. Good. Nothing like a dose of reality to set her feet back on solid ground. She reached for the last button he'd opened.

"Don't." His hands shot out to grab her wrists, pulling her arms over his shoulders and holding them there.

They were face to face. His breath mingled with hers while his hips leaned in to her again. She sucked in a breath, desire simmering in her veins. "We should go before I end up proving my point."

She extricated herself, slipping around him to grab her bag. His hand shot through the strap, and he hauled the backpack over his shoulder. She shot him a wary look but continued on to Rayo, patting his neck and shoulder while she pulled herself together. The hard part was over, now they just had to worry about stumbling over cartel killers.

Andres exhaled. "Grab the horn."

She reached for the saddle horn, eyeing Rayo. While she'd ridden before, it was half a lifetime ago. And she didn't remember that horse being quite as big.

Andres cradled his hands, offering her a boost. Lifting her foot, she tried to shake any debris from the hiking boot before stepping into his palms. She shifted her center of gravity then had a horrible thought. What if she was too heavy? A second later she was several feet off the ground, more than enough clearance to sit astride.

Andres reached for the saddle horn, his arm brushing high on her thigh, sending her pulse skipping ahead. He climbed on behind her. "Move up a little." Her eyes widened as hard thighs slid under hers, and the bulk of his zipper settled in behind her. His chest bumped her shoulder right before his arms came around her. This time the world lurched.

They were spooned together from shoulder to ankle. Warm, hard man to needy, tormented woman. All sorts of fireworks exploded in her lower regions. "Let me..." She swallowed. "How can I...um..."

"Shhh. This is as good as it's gonna get," he whispered by her ear.

His breath flowed over her neck and shoulder, tightening a knot in her chest. Her fingers curled. What should she do with her hands? "I was just told to prepare for rough terrain." She'd thought hiking boots and shrubs.

"And I just knew someone was coming to get him."

Moni grasped at a possible reprieve. "Sh-should we

walk?"

"No." He clicked his tongue, and Rayo started moving. "If he asked for a doctor, he might need help coming out."

Rayo stepped through the grass with barely a sound. For several minutes, they crossed the land in silence. Since Andres seemed to know exactly where they were going, Monica focused her attention on the surroundings. The nearly full moon cast a cold light that illuminated everything in faint purple hues.

They broke out of the brush and approached a cluster of trees. She couldn't help but stare. The river curled blue-black around a lovely sandbar that looked ideal for a sunny afternoon picnic. She shuddered and turned her head away.

He tightened his arm slightly and bent his head to her ear. "This isn't where it happened."

She was relieved. Such a beautiful spot shouldn't be a scene for a horrific multiple murder. "In the old days, women bathed here and the men had a separate area downriver." He went quiet for a moment. "If I'd known you were coming I could have found you a damn vest," he mumbled.

"The backpack is lined with Kevlar."

He swung the pack around, setting the shield before her without missing a beat. "If anything happens, hold it close so you'll be protected." She clutched the handle, holding on like a lifeline.

The hard contours of his chest brushed against her back. "What about you?"

"I'll slow down anything coming in from behind." Reality drained every bit of strength she possessed. She stared over her shoulder at him in disbelief. "It's okay, Doc." He didn't spare her a glance. "We just need to get you in and out in one piece."

"Why didn't you?"

"Bring a vest?"

She nodded.

A smile played at his lips. "It would have been a hard sell to say I was going out to meet a woman if I needed to strap on a vest.

"There's a fair amount of people climbing through bedroom windows in the middle of the night. They just keep things all private like."

What windows had he climbed through? Who was the lucky woman—or women—in his life? Was Lupe right? Had he reunited with Susana? Was she tucked away right now, waiting for him to return? No, he didn't seem the type…but then neither had Valdo. Until she'd found out about the other woman.

Why did she care? It was none of her business who got to use his body as their personal playground.

Crap. She searched the area, trying to find a landmark. Where were they? What direction had he taken?

"What's wrong?"

His breath sent a tingling rush down her neck. She jerked back against his shoulder, drying a damp palm on her jeans. "Nothing."

"Calm down. You're jumpier than a cricket on a busy sidewalk."

How the hell was she supposed to act? Her senses, heightened by lust and edged with fear, were all tuned to him. The heat of his body, the strong arms surrounding her, the hard thighs pressing against hers with every step Rayo took.

"I know you're scared, but you need to try and act natural," he murmured from beside her temple.

Natural. Right. Better he should think she was scared spitless. "Do you think we're being watched?"

"No. Guerrero sent everybody out. But if someone else *is* watching they'll never buy us sneaking around together if you don't relax." His arm settled against her ribs, pulling her back against the warmth of his chest.

That made sense. Still, he was taking her into dangerous territory, on a very personal level. She exhaled, settling back. *Relax. Act natural. Like a woman off to find a secluded spot to have sex.*

"Natural for us is you acting up and me trying to keep from taking you in hand."

His chuckle rushed past her shoulder. "Okay, I admit I like to push your buttons."

"Mmm-hmm."

"You came to town a quiet, scrawny little kid who was all business." Scrawny was right. Months of juggling the wedding arrangements and a high-stress job had left her with all the curves of a med school skeleton.

"You filled in real nice." His hand moved closer to her breast, his thumb brushing the underside. "I like making you smile and blush." His lips teased the shell of her ear, sending a dusting of sparks down her body. "But nothing compares to your deadly stare. You're alive and fiery. Almost as beautiful as when you've been thoroughly kissed."

This was the wrong night for confessions. They were on the way to help someone, but all she could think about was the attention her body was clamoring for. "You were such a jerk. I wanted to wring your neck so many times."

He chuckled. "Sometimes you looked like you were going to knock me on my ass."

Lord knew she'd wanted to.

"Sometimes I hoped you'd follow me down," he finished in a quieter tone.

Yes, sometimes she'd wanted that, too. They could end up tangled together, and she could finally see if that image of him moving over her would live up to the real thing.

His lips trailed down the shell of her ear, and she had to swallow a needy whimper. Her lids drifted closed, allowing her senses to bask in the pleasure of being caressed by the man who'd taken up residence in her most private thoughts. She brought her jaw higher, letting his hot breath fan across her skin. The fine hair at the base of her neck stood on end. Sensation cascaded down her arms and legs. His thighs cupped her bottom, and the hard ridge reaching her lower back had her sex contracting. She leaned into him, seeking him over her shoulder. "Andres…" Her breasts were heavy, the nipples puckering painfully, needing more.

His mouth came down on hers and he cradled her breast. She brought her hand up to stop him, but he wouldn't budge. Instead, he pinched the stiff nipple between two fingers. She couldn't stifle the moan that erupted from her throat while her back arched into his grasp.

He tore his mouth from hers, looking down to see how she filled his hand. "When we're done here," — his gravelly voice struck a chord in her. He was as affected as she was — "I'm going to strip off those cock-teasing jeans and spread you out on a blanket so I can taste every inch of you." His hand slid down her body. Her eyes widened, knowing she had to put a stop to this now.

"Wh-what about Susana?"

He went stock-still, unwilling to believe the words he'd just heard. She knew…

"We're not together—" He stopped himself before adding "anymore." How could he have thought she wouldn't know? Since coming home he'd kept to himself, rarely communicating with anyone outside of the ranch. Somehow the tactic had backfired. Nobody really knew the man he'd become. They all remembered the wild kid he'd been.

The wind caught her silky black hair, sending the long

strands against his bicep. Her scent surrounded him, a fragrance as subtle as the woman herself—at least when it came to anyone but him. He'd tortured himself with the taste of her, the freedom she'd allowed him over her body. His mouth watered. His hands itched to touch all of her—an indulgence he should know better than to permit himself. But he didn't want to fight it anymore. He wanted her, more than he'd ever wanted any woman.

She was nothing if not precise and efficient. All she had to say were three little words, and every bit of desire heating his blood trickled out of his system. Fuck. And he'd been worried about some asshole jumping them from the shadows.

They rode the next half mile in strained silence, Monica resting against him. "How did you end up a part of all this?"

"Damian reached out to me."

"*Damian*?" Her head shot back, narrowly missing his chin.

Good God. She hadn't known who she was meeting or who she was going to treat. It was a wonder she was alive.

"His boss checked up on me and told him I was okay."

"Tonight?"

"No." He drew in a deep breath as they covered the last few yards. "I've been feeding him information the last few months." And he'd spent too many nights wondering if he was gonna end up dead on the side of some road. But up until now Damian had been straight with him.

"That's dangerous."

"So is showing up to meet someone in the middle of the night," he reasoned. "At least I'm doing it to get my ranch back. Why are you?" She clamped her mouth shut and faced forward.

He reined in Rayo, making sure they were at the right spot. "Wait here." He passed her the reins then dismounted. His whistle—one short, one long, in quick succession—was answered with two short bursts. "We're good."

She handed down her pack before swinging her leg around. He barely had time to grab her waist...and appreciate her nicely rounded, heart-shaped bottom. Since he'd known her, she'd always been wearing heels. Tonight, in kid-sized hiking boots, her head barely reached his shoulder.

She pulled back her hair then, typical of her nature, held out her hands for the backpack. His eyebrow shot up. The damn thing weighed more than she did. Instead, he unstrapped the blanket and offered her the bundle.

A grin pulled at the corners of his mouth. He didn't need to see her face to know she was giving him one of those dirty looks. How could pissing off a woman get a man hard?

"Come on. He's up ahead." Backtracking, he whispered to Rayo, "You stay put. I don't plan on walking all the way back."

The damn horse nickered softly and dropped his head, seeking something to graze on—effectively blowing him off. "I'm gonna have you made into glue if you don't mind me."

His attention turned to the rocky ground barely illuminated by moonlight. A few yards and Damian came into view, watching from a natural shelf created by two larger rocks. He was naked, one arm folded against his chest like a broken wing, a dark smear trailing down from his shoulder.

Monica hit doctor mode, hurrying ahead to kneel next to her patient. Andres set the backpack down, studying the hard angles of Damian's jaw. Doc moved the blanket out of the way, flipped the bag and opened a zipper, producing snack bars and a water bottle. "Here. Eat slowly."

"Thanks." Damian offered up his arm, grimacing as she went to work. He grabbed the water, biting the cap as he twisted the bottle open.

Andres glanced back and forth between them. Was he the only one having a problem with Damian being naked? "The blanket has some pants in it."

Damian reached for the bundle Doc had set behind her. "Think I can get these clothes on first?"

"They can wait." Monica rummaged through her bag. He slumped back, struggling with the snack bar wrapper.

Talking Monica Vasquez away from her purpose was as easy as freezing in August. "Let her finish, man. She's relentless." He probably got another dirty look for his two cents.

"I need to turn on a light."

Andres grabbed the blanket off the ground. "I'll hold this up to block the light." While they faced away from the road, someone might still see a bright spot floating on the side of the mountain. He unrolled the bundle, tossing Damian the jeans he'd brought along.

The light turned on, dim enough not to give away their location.

"The bullet went in by my shoulder blade and came out the front."

"That's an accurate assessment."

He grunted. "I've built a decent medical file."

"So I see," Doc murmured.

Andres leaned the base of his palms against the outcropping, draping the blanket against the boulders on either side. Lucky for Damian, the rocks held some of the day's heat. If he'd been stranded without shelter, he wouldn't have done as well. Tonight's breeze carried a little bite.

Rustling, a clink, more rustling, and a mumbled curse escaped from behind the curtain. Andres cleared his throat. "What happened the other night?"

"I'm not even sure. Sometime after midnight, Paloma decided she wanted to go swimming," Damian said around a mouthful. "We tried talking her out of it, but she took off running. We caught up to her at the river and eventually ended up at one of the swimming holes." Damian stopped, swigging more water.

"And you got ambushed?"

"N-no. I think the bastard watched us for a while. Couldn't tell. We were skinny-dipping, and Paloma was splashing around, laughing. Then she…wanted attention." Score one for town gossip. "Lalo was on watch, but he was having trouble focusing."

"He ended up with his throat slit."

"Yeah." He exhaled. "I figured. I heard gagging but I thought Paloma—"

"Gagging?" Doc's radar kicked in.

"Yeeeeah. She was giving Capo head."

"I see."

Andres grinned at her reaction then sobered as he recalled the scene he'd found. "So you didn't see the shooter?"

"No, dude. Paloma was on me."

"Do you know how many guys attacked?"

"One, I think. Fffu…" He muttered under his breath. "It… She wasn't sitting on my cock, man." He'd painted a good enough picture. "I heard the shots. *Vato* used a silencer— maybe Lalo's gun. Paloma went limp on me, then Capo hit the ground. I pushed her off…and took one to the shoulder when I got up."

Andres looked around. "At least you got out."

"I had no cover and nowhere to go but the river." His voice went tight. "Luckily there was enough current to help carry me around the bend before I had to come up for air. When I got to safety, I walked around for hours trying to find this place. Figured my best bet was to get to the SAT phone we'd hidden."

"Let's see your feet," Doc instructed.

They shuffled around behind the blanket trying to get into position. He checked the surroundings, as a precaution.

Guerrero thought Damian had taken off, so he'd sent men out instead of setting up guards. Damian wasn't the shooter. So who was killing everyone? Had the chief stumbled onto something, or had he been a target along with the cartel?

Dr. Treviño had confided in him earlier in the day, sharing details about the scene. He wouldn't tell Damian about Capo's castration in front of Doc. The killer had shoved the pieces in Paloma's mouth. What kind of an animal did that to a woman? What message was he trying to send Guerrero?

"This will keep until you can get to a hospital." The light flipped off.

"Thanks. I guess Angel knew what he was doing."

Doc packed her bag and got up, dusting off her butt while she held a small package tucked under her chin. "He's been right a time or two."

"Yeah, I'm so fucking glad he found you two, or I'd probably be dead." Moni looked over at him. Andres realized he knew nothing about this "Angel" other than the fact that Damian and Monica trusted him. Was that really good enough? Where was he getting his background information? He dropped his arms and found Damian struggling into his jeans.

"Gimme a second to get these pants on." Damian grunted, trying to get dressed behind the curtain.

Andres put the blanket back in place, giving the guy a little privacy. "Hope they fit okay."

"Yeah, they're good." He zipped the jeans.

Monica tore open the plastic wrapping and unrolled a triangular cloth. "He lost a good deal of blood. I'm surprised he made it up the mountain in this condition."

In other words, Damian wasn't going to make it out on his own.

"Fuck," he said from the enclosure. "Even my ass is sunburned."

Andres folded the blanket back into a tight roll while Damian hobbled to his feet. "You should have asked for shoes."

"Didn't even think about them. I wanted to backtrack to the ranch and try to grab some supplies, but I had no idea who jumped us."

Doc stuffed the packaging in a baggie then removed her gloves and tossed them in without making a sound. He was starting to wonder about the little doctor. Tonight had been an eye-opener. How had she ended up called in for this? He'd assumed she was a second stringer, like him. But now he wasn't so sure. He'd agreed to work with Damian to try and get his ranch back. Why would she put herself at risk when she didn't even know who she was risking her life for? And why had she closed up when he asked her about it? Anger roiled within him. Angel. The guy had to be some little pencil pusher who'd never been face to face with the cartel. Did he even realize the danger he'd put Monica in?

"Trust me, you made the right choice." Andres jerked off the buttoned shirt he wore over his dark T-shirt for Damian to wear. "Guerrero thinks you're the shooter. He's got people looking for you."

"They came by the office," she added. "And from what I've heard, they went around town, too."

"Okay." He winced, pulling on a sleeve. "What'd he set up?"

"They figured you took off, so he sent the guys to Monterrey and San Luis."

Doc tied the ends of the triangle together then looped the sling over his neck. Damian set his arm inside, adjusting until he found a comfortable angle. "Thanks for the heads-up." He held out his hand. Andres took it—it was probably the most humbling experience the guy'd ever had. "I'm being pulled out anyway. I'll see what Angel decides to do."

His stomach sank. Helping Damian and his people had been the one chance at undermining Guerrero and getting the ranch back. "Is that it? Is everything getting shut down?"

Damian shook his head. "No. We're in too deep to drop everything."

"So what else can I do? I don't want to have to start from scratch."

"You just keep doing what you're doing. I'll leave you the SAT phone. Angel will reach out and tell you who to hand it to."

"But there has to be some —"

"Dude, you have no idea just how much you've done." He shook his head. "I'm probably going to get my ass handed to me, but what the fuck. If Angel said you could be trusted." He shrugged. "With your info we've figured out who's paying off Guerrero instead of actually running horses. Those trackers you've set up have helped map out their network into the States. You have no idea how deep this goes."

"You know this is to get my place back."

"Angel is working on backtracking so he can bring Guerrero down. Then you can get everything back. But you have to realize how fucking methodical this guy is."

"All right." But he didn't know how much patience he'd have left.

"Just hang tight. It'll happen."

"Thanks, man. Hope it works out for you, too." Andres looked out at the night as they started across the rocky terrain. He'd been 'hanging tight' since taking the job with Guerrero. He'd taken a huge chance trusting that Damian was who he said he was. The last few months would test any man's nerves, and he'd more than held up his part of the bargain. He tucked away his disappointment and focused on the task at hand. They still had a long way to go.

"I'm guessing your people don't know what condition

you're really in."

Damian looked from him to Doc. "Didn't seem too bad when I got here."

"Adrenaline kept you going," Doc explained.

"Yeah, well, you never mentioned needing a doctor. And you said I was bringing in someone to pick you up."

"Fuck." Damian rubbed the back of his neck.

"More details would have helped. Now we're a little tight on the ride." Regardless of how he switched everyone around, there was no safe way to get them all out. "Doc, you and Damian ride on ahead. I'll follow on foot."

Damian's eyes widened as they walked back to the horse. "I don't know how to drive that thing." Rayo flipped his tail in disapproval.

Doc shook her head. "I doubt I'd do any better if things went wrong." She looked up at him. "I think you'd better take him."

Every instinct rebelled. She couldn't be serious. "I'm not leaving you here."

"You need to get him out. Now. I'll catch up, but I need you to drop off my bag."

"Shit. I'm not liking this." Damian's eyes narrowed, checking out Monica.

"I have the shoes and pants for a hike."

Andres looked her up and down. Sure enough, she'd prepared for this trip—better than he had. His head told him her plan made sense. The rest of him shouted a loud, clear protest. If she thought he could justify leaving a tiny slip of a woman miles from the fence line all by herself, she was nuts.

"I'll be fine." She nodded toward Damian. "Besides, I'm not a target. He is."

"Did you bring any weapons?" Damian's hopeful tone intruded.

Yeah, pile on more, why don't you? I can feel worse than

crap. His presence was barely tolerated at the ranch. No way he'd be allowed a weapon, even for snakes.

"Here." Doc unzipped a side pouch on her bag. They watched as she pulled out a gun, running her fingers over the safety before handing it to Damian. "Nine millimeter. Loaded. Safety's on. Two magazines in the pouch." His jaw dropped. Who the hell was this woman?

Damian flashed his teeth in a grin. "You're all right, lady doc."

"Someone very special gave me that gun. I want it back," she said in her "doctor's orders" tone.

"God—" Andres bit off his words and turned to Damian. "Get on the damn horse." Damian glared at him before limping to Rayo's right side. *For fuck's sake.* "Other side." Andres went around Rayo and grabbed his bridle. "How the hell have you managed to be at the ranch this long and never learn to ride?"

Holding the strap with his good hand, Damian lifted his foot awkwardly and stuck it into the metal stirrup, wincing as he reached for the saddle horn. He leaned his forehead against the leather before taking a deep breath, then hoisted himself up onto the saddle, landing with a thud. Rayo skittered sideways, ears flattened against the unfamiliar rider. Damian swayed, muttering curses as he grabbed at Rayo's mane and anything else he could find to hold.

"Easy amigo, don't go loco on me now," Andres murmured, soothing the horse to a standstill before glancing up at Damian, who looked nervous for the first time since he'd met the man. "You gonna make it?"

"That's why I don't ride; a car would never pull that shit on you." He glanced at the ground. "If I fall off just leave me there, not climbing back up here again."

Andres shook his head as he handed the bag up to him while he worked through scenarios. Damian should have told him about the shape he was in. He turned to Monica. "We're gonna need your car to take him farther out."

"I can drive him. No use exposing you any more than necessary." Typical. She thought about everyone but herself. He racked his brain for an alternative. "We're probably better off leading Rayo and having him ride on his own. Let's start walking while we figure out the rest." She held out her hand, looking like a kid—sweet and innocent—instead of the woman he knew her to be.

He dug his heels in. "Doc, nothing you can say will convince me he's better off on that horse by himself."

"You're probably right." The way she looked up through her lashes should have been his first warning. "Help me up, into his lap." Uh... He clamped his mouth shut, fighting the jealousy spearing through him. She shifted, jutting her hip out as she turned. The tempting view down her blouse drew his gaze. "I think I'll do okay with the reins. He'll just have to hold on tight."

His hand clamped around her bicep. "Oh, hell no."

"Still think you're right?" she teased.

"Take your time. I'll try not to bleed to death while I'm waiting," Damian growled.

Doc glared at Damian as Andres led her away, a hand at the back of her waist.

Damian looked from one to the other. "You know, we're going to pass by a motel..." He left the words hanging.

Andres grabbed the reins. There was no way Monica was going off with him on her own. He'd drive Damian wherever he needed to go, but the son of a bitch would ride in the trunk.

Chapter Eight

The staccato click of high heels on linoleum followed Moni down the hallway to the side door. She'd been upstairs, at her kitchen window, keeping an eye out for Andres to return with her car. Lupe was arriving early today since Simon would be tied up with inventory at the store. She didn't want them meeting up accidentally and having to answer Lupe's questions on why Andres was here without Dr. Treviño.

Andres had followed them on Rayo, leaving him tied up just outside of town. She'd been dropped off at home and left to worry. Sunrise wasn't too far away, and he'd lose the cover of darkness. She'd been at the point of biting her nails when she spotted the car coming around the corner.

Releasing her ponytail from under her coat's collar, she pulled open the door to find him on the doorstep. "Thank God you made it."

His step slowed and his gaze traveled down the front of her teal dress with undisguised interest. It was a little shorter than what she usually wore, barely peeking out under her white coat. "I'm fine, Doc."

"So I hear." He took the two steps up to the door and continued in, making her step back.

"Were you worried about me or the car?" he asked, pulling the door back until the knob slipped from her hold.

She gave him a dirty look. "My patient."

His lips quirked at one corner. "Of course. I should have known." He held his index finger straight, the key ring hanging off his knuckle. She should grab the keys and walk him out. Lupe would be here any time now. But she'd caught the almost imperceptible wince at the answer she'd lobbed him. Truth be told, he'd been on her mind all night. He'd risked his own life to get Kris's man out of town while she tossed and turned—in the safety of her bed—for the past few hours. Though that was far from being the only reason.

She looked up at him through her lashes. "Maybe I worried about you, too...a little."

He placed his hand over his chest, tapping his fingers as if his heart had gone aflutter. "Was that so hard?"

"No." She fought a grin. "I guess not."

He ran his knuckles along her chin. "Maybe you could think of me more often."

If only he knew how much time she spent thinking about him instead of the task at hand. "I don't think that's possible."

He leaned in, his hat brim blocking the light, to brush his lips over hers. Heartbeat racing, she caught his bottom lip between hers, watching him watch her with naked desire. He slanted his mouth over hers, deepening the contact. Slipping his hands around her hips, he backed her against the wall, wedging his leg between hers in the process. Long fingers stretched down her sides then raked back up to her waist. His knee made it under the hem of her dress, sliding against the sensitive skin of her inner thighs.

Last night she'd felt off-kilter when he'd taken over her personal space. Now, in familiar surroundings, she craved having him against hers. The pleasure he'd drawn from her had her body humming in anticipation. Desperate fingers dug into the hair at his nape, bringing him closer. His tongue plunged into her mouth as he brought them flush against each other.

Her soft moan drew him to her breasts, palming their weight, rolling the stiff nipples while his tongue entwined with hers. Lord, his cock was deliciously hard, offering promises that had her senses clamoring in response. The slow, agonizing twist of her hips brought his thigh against one of hers, then the other. He shifted with her, moving them into the adjoining exam room.

He nibbled at the corner of her lips, then at her chin. His hat toppled off, falling to the floor without notice as he trailed toward her neck. Another step and he had her balanced on the edge of the exam table. Tightening her grip on his shoulders, she steadied herself. "Andres…" The seam of his jeans brushed past the top of her thigh-highs. His thumbs explored the flowers trimming the elastic lace, teasing the sensitive skin they covered. She bit back a whimper. A couple more inches and he'd be at her panties, find them drenched.

He tugged up the hem of her dress, while his teeth raked down her neck and across her shoulder. The cool air nipping at her back did nothing to cool the fire he had lit inside her. Still she waited, her entire body shuddering under his touch, her grasp tightening on his shoulders.

"What are you doing to me?" The words were barely a whisper off his lips. Glazed eyes studied her features in the dim light. "All I can think about is seeing you. Touching you. Tasting you." His fingers reached her apex, strumming across the damp material. "I want to make you as crazy as you make me, so hot you forget about everything except screaming my name when you come." With a rush of his breath he lowered his forehead to hers.

Lips parted, she marveled at the panting breaths echoing between them. Her hips moved against him without any conscious thought on her part, begging for more. He willingly obliged, slipping under the damp silk to explore.

An unexpected jolt ran through her body, rippling with every stroke of his searching fingers. "Lie back." She stretched out, letting the coat she still wore drop open, displaying the fitted bodice of her dress. The sight caught his attention. He pushed his finger past her slit, and his mouth closed over her nipple, straight through the dress.

A cry broke past her lips at the unexpected caress. He answered with a firm nip before retreating. *Dios*, he was going to kill her. With one quick tug he removed the lacy black panties. The table creaked when he settled in. "I need more room." He lifted her left leg over his shoulder.

Frustration clenched her sex. "Uh-uh." He ran his lips over her, and she was suddenly glad she'd taken up waxing. She could feel every touch, reveling in the distinction between bare skin and the areas still sparsely covered. He ran his tongue over her slit, coming back to nibble at her, right above where she needed him.

Her breath rushed out and she bit her lip, wanting him to do it again, following through this time. His tongue dipped in, right over her entrance, and moved up her body, slipping out right before he reached her clitoris. Her legs tensed, moving restlessly around him as he started the exquisite torture all over again. She angled her hips, trying to position herself just right, but his tongue slid down, then started over again, teasing her into moving.

"That's right, sweetheart. Move for me." A harsh breath rushed out, understanding what he wanted. "Ride my tongue like you rode against my cock." The things he said... But her body obeyed him, mimicking the motion from last night while he rewarded her with delicious pressure. Her muscles tightened and he thrust two fingers inside her, shattering the tenuous hold on her self-control. Her legs spread farther and he clamped down on her clitoris, sucking her in.

The cry echoing in the room was her...she knew that somewhere in a corner of her mind. And she must have arched off the table, because her back landed with a firm thud, then her legs went limp around his shoulders. She looked down her body to make sure he was all right after having three-inch heels digging into him.

The sight of him stopped her. Their eyes locked, his deep and intense, scorching her with need. Anticipation claimed her again. He wanted her, and she could scarcely breathe with the sudden need to have him fill her. She squeezed her inner muscles around his fingers.

"Fuck, baby. You're so damn tight. We may need to go again before I can get my cock inside you without hurting you."

She groaned deep in her throat; settling back, she let her lids drift shut, enjoying his intimate touch. If this had brought her to the most powerful orgasm she'd ever experienced, what would he manage with—

"It's safe to come in, *Mamá*. The office is empty."

Her eyes popped open as she rose on her elbows. "Simon...Lu-Lupe." Desire drained at the reality of the situation. The skirt she'd painstakingly ironed was bunched up at her waist. One of her legs was still curled over a man's shoulder and her dress bore a wet spot over her nipple from his earlier attention. She uncurled her legs from around him and wiggled off the table as he straightened.

Shaking hands smoothed down her dress then dragged her coat closed before fumbling with the buttons. "You need to go." He was inordinately quiet, his mouth barely a slash on his face. How could he be upset? He wasn't the one standing there on unsteady legs wondering what the hell happened to his panties while people were walking toward them.

She ducked her head to go past him. He caught her arm, whirling her around. His hand dug into her hair, pulling her back to face him right before his lips came down on hers.

His mouth dominated hers, pushing past her lips to claim her all over again. She brought her hand up to his shoulder, aiming to push him away, but couldn't follow through. She tasted herself on his mouth and the chaos churning within her collapsed.

He held the back of her head, but her entire body responded, melting against him. Andres released her, but she wasn't sure her legs could support her. Her body ached for him to be inside her with an intensity she'd never experienced.

Panting, she cradled his face. "I'm sorry…" Swallowing, she shook her head. He was still hard, and she was going to leave him wanting yet again. "I didn't… She was coming in early."

"Go." He nodded toward the door. She didn't move. Could she throw caution to the wind and meet him upstairs? Would she even bother to sneak around or be quiet? Lupe would tell the whole town before she had his boots off. He must have seen the doubt in her eyes, because he dropped a quick kiss on her temple. "Go. You'll need to distract them while I straighten up in here and slip out."

Tamping down the disappointment, she turned and forced her feet to move. With one last glance over her shoulder, she went around the doorframe and into the hall.

R ayo trotted up the drive, heading straight for the stable. They'd had a nice long ride, but nothing was getting Andres past the hard-on he'd had most of the night. The image of Monica, hazel eyes heavy-lidded after her orgasm, was stuck in his head. She'd squeezed down on his fingers and his dick—

"Seriously." Lourdes stepped out of shadows. "You chose last night to stay out till morning."

Rayo stopped by the tack room, ready to be unsaddled. "And good morning to you, ma'am." Andres dismounted then dutifully reached for the cinch. What was she up to? In the years she'd been a housekeeper, she'd never spent any of her spare time in the stable.

"That good or that far?"

"Excuse me?"

"You've never stayed out all night when you used to *go riding*. So I figure this girl was either that good or she lived pretty far."

Although they'd been friends for most of their lives, he couldn't believe she'd gone there. "The *girls* I messed around with, when I was a *kid*, are all married or gone." He took a deep breath, trying to settle down before the horse picked up on his annoyance.

"So it must be someone who lives far. Because I can't think of anyone you'd be messing around with in town."

This was the wrong time to make that observation. In fact, he had half a mind to turn it around on her and ask how she ended up with hay in her braid.

"Did you need something, or you just here to bust my ass?"

She had the decency to look embarrassed. He lifted the saddle and placed it on a rack. "Actually…"

Back stiff, he walked right past her and led Rayo to his stall.

"I'm sorry, Andresito. I fell asleep waiting for you and ended up with a stiff neck. Now I'm in a bad mood."

Crap. She musta been waiting a while. "What did you need?" he asked, throwing off his annoyance.

"Morning." Two of the ranch hands filed in, calling out their greeting.

"Morning, guys."

"Good morning," she added quietly.

He waited, but she just watched the men start their chores. "Lulu." He reverted to her nickname. "Are you okay?"

"Yeah." She pasted on a smile. "Any chance...do you think you might be going to town today?"

"I don't know yet."

"Okay. Well, can you—"

Alex walked in and they exchanged greetings.

"So..." Lourdes shoved her hand in her pocket. "Can you tell me once you know?"

"Yeah, I can do that." Andres frowned. "You sure you're okay?"

She gave him that same fake smile. "I just have a lot of stuff to do. I better get back." She pointed a thumb toward the house and took off.

Alex came up behind him. "What was that about?"

Andres shook his head as both men watched her return to the main house. "I have no idea."

Lupe sat in the front office, hunched over a file while Dora buffed her nails. Monica leaned against the doorway, a big cup of coffee in hand. Her eyelids begged for a few stolen moments to nap after her midnight run with Andres and Damian.

She'd be okay if she was busy, but the waiting area was empty, same as yesterday. With fear taking over the town after the chief's death, they'd likely have an empty office every afternoon. "Are you almost done for the day?"

"No." Lupe's curt answer drew Dora's startled gaze.

She immediately bent her neck, her back going unnaturally straight. Discreetly, she set the nail buffer she'd been using into the nearest drawer.

Monica stared at the ceiling. *Please give me patience.* "I'd be happy to pitch in," she offered, "so you ladies can be home before the sun goes down."

Lupe swiveled in the chair, giving her a pointed look. "I'm glad you brought that up. This new schedule you've implemented has to change."

Moni looked from her to Dora. The younger woman's shoulders shot up, her eyes wide and baffled.

"I haven't implemented any schedule, Lupe." Had the older woman not realized what was going on around her? "If there's a problem with you getting home, I can give you a ride."

Her lips tightened. "People are starting to whisper. They're asking how I could be done for the day so early now that you're in charge of the office. When Dr. Treviño was here I was working until all hours." Her chin dipped and her eyes shifted to Dora, then back. "It's embarrassing." Her entire face took on a rosy hue.

Dora pressed her lips together, her teeth capturing them as she swiveled her chair to face away from them. Her shoulders shook, but she managed to not utter a sound.

"I didn't realize." Would she ever get used to dealing with etiquette from a century gone by? "People are staying off the streets at night. With everything that's happened, I think closing mid-afternoon is a good idea."

Lupe rolled the pen between her fingers, looking like a fish out of water.

"How about I treat you both to an early dinner so we can unwind? Afterward, I can drop you off."

Dora grinned and readily agreed to the offer.

Lupe wasn't quite so enthusiastic. "If you're sure."

Moni nodded.

"We'd have to discuss work if people are around. I don't want anyone thinking we're getting too friendly," she added.

Not many would come to such a silly conclusion. "I'm sure Dora and I will do our best to follow your lead."

"Yes, ma'am." Dora agreed.

Lupe checked her watch. "Simon should be done with work soon." A smile softened her features. "I'll call him to join us."

Great. Just what she needed, another session of sitting between Lupe and her son while she was matchmaking.

"Oh." Dora's face lit up. "You think he'd come?"

"He'd be thrilled to join the doctor for dinner."

Dora's smile faltered.

Monica dumped out her coffee then returned to the office and shrugged off her coat. Hmmm. So Dora was the lure for Simon's frequent office visits. She hadn't seen that one coming. With a little creativity, she might be able to make the best of this unexpected piece of information.

A ndres looked into the stable to make sure the grooms were occupied. Heart pounding, he pulled up the cup holder on the truck's rear passenger door and dropped in a tracker.

"What are you doing?" Lourdes snapped, poking her head through the driver's side window.

"*Shit!*" Andres swore, his heart almost exploding in his chest. He dropped the cup holder, pressing his eyes closed as he dragged in a deep, calming breath.

She came around the truck. "You were supposed to tell me if you had a trip into town," she hissed, planting her hands on her wide hips.

"I don't." He nodded at Alex, who was heading down the path from his cabin. "Alex is taking Bailarina to Monterrey."

"Oh." Her shoulders drooped.

"Dr. Treviño's supposed to get with you to see—"

"You told him?" she squeaked. Her dark skin went pale, and she grabbed her apron, rolling it into a ball at her stomach.

He shut the door, coming around to check on her. "I-I... You didn't say not to tell him anything."

"I didn't tell you to go ask him, either," she shot back with annoyance.

"I'd have to ask him. He's the reason I go to town." Damn, he must have ruined her plan. "I'm sorry, Lulu. I didn't know I was supposed to keep things on the down-low."

Lourdes dropped the apron, bringing her hands to her temples as she released a heavy breath.

"Well, can Alex get whatever you need from Monterrey?"

"No, Alex can't," he said as he shot straight past them, heading for the stalls.

She dug her chin against her chest, quickly shaking her head, as if she wanted him to drop it.

"What the hell?" He glared over his shoulder at Alex, then turned back to Lourdes. Was everyone going nuts? His tired mind raced, trying to piece together what happened.

She looked over her shoulder at the house before turning back to him. "I'll find you later on," she said quietly, then turned to leave.

Alex stalked back to the trailer, leading Bailarina by the reins. "What did you tell the old man to have him send me out instead of you?"

"I didn't say anything." Andres stopped Alex, pulling the reins from his hand. "If it bothers you so much, tell him you won't go." Bailarina sidestepped, conscious of the tension between the men. She wasn't happy being pulled out of her stall to begin with. "I have no problem making the drive."

Alex cocked his head, glaring at him. "Why not, man? You can even swing by and pick up the little doc on the way, right? So you don't get lonely in Monterrey, all by yourself."

Andres glanced behind him to make sure none of the grooms followed him out of the stable. Their personal issues were nobody else's business. "Yeah," he mocked. "I'm sure she'd be ready to drop everything and jump in the truck. What woman wouldn't get all hot and bothered about hauling a horse trailer across the state? *Pendejo*."

Alex was pissed over something else. He'd never complained about making a run to Monterrey. Then again, this wasn't a regular errand. Dr. Treviño had asked him to take Bailarina in to have her mane and tail dyed back to the original color. The constant reminder of Paloma was causing Guerrero some health problems. The boss had been drunk or pissed or both for days. Who could blame the man, after finding his kid in pieces?

"What is it with you and doctors? You're trying to get under one's skirt and having a bromance with the other." He tipped his chin up, taunting him.

"Screw you." Andres held Bailarina as she shook her head, pulling away. He had to get her in the trailer before she tried heading to the stable. "And while we're talking about doctors, the shit you said to Monica was outta line, *vato*. What happened between you and I stays here. She's never done anything to have you disrespect her."

Alex's lips tightened for a second then his shoulders dropped. "Yeah...I fucked up. I'll talk to her."

"No." He shook his head, his upper lip curling. "No talking. You'll apologize to her."

"Yeah, I'll apologize. I was an ass; she didn't deserve that." He plopped against the truck while Andres coaxed Bailarina into the trailer. "I'm gonna be stuck waiting on the prig hairdresser." Alex slammed the base of his fist against the side of the truck.

"Yeah, payback's a bitch." The guy would keep Alex waiting on him because he enjoyed the attention. Nothing like having a captive audience to hit on or flirt with. Andres locked Bailarina in, giving her a final pat. He was frustrated; people were pissed at him for shit he had no control over. "So what's the big deal?"

"They're having some fancy dinner tonight, and I'm gonna miss it over this shit."

Damn. If Lourdes was planning a surprise, she should have said so. Was today the doctor's birthday? Or some other special occasion? Nobody told him anything around here. All this crap over a frickin' dinner. The way the day had gone, it had better be the dinner to end all dinners.

"I just don't get why Bailarina has to go in *today*," Alex complained. "It's like Dr. Treviño doesn't want me around."

"Hey, I didn't know they're having a thing tonight, either." Andres shrugged. Not that he'd be included in anything happening in his childhood home. "You're already screwed. Stay the night and come back tomorrow."

Alex's shoulder twitched and he shook his head. "No can do." His gaze skidded back to the main house. "He's having me take Susana and the baby." Andres's stomach tightened. *Crap*. They'd be stuck together for hours. Alex and the woman who'd made a fool of him. Much as he tried, he'd never found a good time to clear the air.

"He gave me a load of cash," Alex continued, "and said to get them clothes, a crib, a car seat, and whatever else she needed for the kid."

The news shouldn't have surprised him. Dr. Treviño was a generous man, yet it bugged him, especially when it came to doling out favors to Susana. As soon as she arrived he'd settled her into the Calderon's family home with him, Guerrero, and Paloma. Somehow he didn't think Susana had been bunking with Maria and Lourdes, by the kitchen. How had he gotten Guerrero to agree to everything? How much say did Dr. Treviño have?

Andres pulled off his hat and slapped it a few times against his thigh, shedding the day's dust off the leather. Alex was his best friend, and it was his fault that a woman had come between them. He rolled the rim back into shape. This would be the perfect time for him to make amends, to finally explain to Alex how things had gone so wrong, so quickly.

"Listen Alex, I've been…"

"I'm ready, Alex. We should get going. I have a lot of things to pick up." Susana strolled up, baby in her arms, as if it were the most natural thing in the world for her to be standing between the two men whose friendship she had helped royally screw up. She looked at Andres, her gaze sliding down to his scuffed boots, then back up to his face, assessing and dismissing him in a single glance. Turning back to Alex, she handed him a bag with blankets and the top of a bottle sticking out. "This needs to go into the truck."

Alex took the bag gingerly, and before either man could say a word, she swept past both to the passenger side of the truck, where she waited.

Alex stared at the bag like it held a rattlesnake instead of a rattle. What did two bachelors know about babies? Taking pity on him, Andres leaned in and whispered, "Pretty sure it's just bottles and diapers, you know, for the kid." Alex's shoulders slumped. He looked at Andres.

"You were gonna say something?"

"Alex? I'm waiting. Can you come open the door so we can go?" Both men closed their eyes, and Andres silently cursed. The moment was gone thanks once again to Susana.

"We'll talk later. It's probably best you get on the road." Andres hesitated a moment, then reached out, grabbing Alex's shoulder and giving a sympathetic squeeze. Alex nodded, then pulled away, walking around to open the door for Susana. He helped her in, waited while she arranged the child in her lap, then handed her the bag, still held at arms' length with two fingers. Andres dropped his head and cleared his throat, trying not to laugh as Susana snatched it from him with a muttered comment.

"You'll have to go slow—"

"I know. I'll be careful." As Alex stomped back around the trailer he glared at Andres, stabbing a finger at him. "Not one word from you, *pendejo*, not one…fucking…word."

Andres stepped back, holding up both hands as Alex yanked open the door, swung into the truck, and slammed it. The small wail that filled the air was immediately drowned out by Susana's shrill voice reading Alex the riot act.

It would have been easy to laugh, but Andres knew this was a "There but for the grace of God" moment for him. As he watched the trailer pull away, he made a silent promise. One way or another, he would find a way to explain to Alex, and to apologize for all that had happened.

Simon arrived at the café, closing the door with excitement in his eyes. He reached the table in a few quick steps. "Ladies, please forgive me." He shot Dora a glance before taking a seat. "I was delayed at the office."

Moni stifled a yawn, dismissing the need for an apology with a wave of her hand. Dora gave him a shy smile. Lupe's face lit up, transforming her from a grouchy busybody to a loving mother within a heartbeat.

The waitress arrived, balancing their plates on a wide tray. "I ordered for you," Lupe said in a giddy schoolgirl tone. "Liver and onions. Your favorite."

Simon's smile didn't reach beyond his lips. Hmm. Maybe

she wasn't the only one to put up with Lupe's personality. Different set of emotions, same end result.

Moni cut into the beef-smothered enchilada plate.

"I realize this isn't proper dinner conversation." Simon placed his napkin on his lap with an apologetic glance around the table. "So please stop me if you're offended."

"Nonsense. I raised you with impeccable manners."

"What happened?" Dora looked up at him through her lashes.

"We had military personnel arrive before I could leave the store. They came next door, since the chief's office is closed." Everyone stopped. Even the group next to them paused, their utensils and drinks frozen in midair. "They were trying to find someone to identify a body."

Lupe splayed her hand over her throat. "Will the tragedies never end?"

Dora's grip tightened around her drink, her eyes wide and incredulous. "Do you know who it was?"

"His face was pretty beat up, but I think he was with Paloma Guerrero at the rodeo."

Dora gasped. "The tattooed man Mr. Guerrero's men asked about."

Moni fought the urge to squirm in her seat. Doubt bounced around inside her like a kernel of popcorn in hot oil. Was it possible? Andres had driven Damian out of town. He'd left the car downstairs in the morning, the weapon tucked under the seat, but they'd never actually discussed the events. A memory tickled the back of her brain. He'd said he was getting rid of them, a few at a time. What exactly had he meant by that?

"I guess now we know why they were asking about him." Two men, known to work for Guerrero, had come by to ask, same as Dr. Treviño.

"Did they say what happened?" Dora whispered.

"One of the soldiers stayed behind. He said…" Simon leaned in and lowered his voice to match hers. "They found him without any clothes on." He unrolled the utensils and used the napkin to blot his forehead. "They believe he was forced to run for his life before or after getting shot. He was thrown in the river so the current would take the body."

"Is that so?" For all she knew, she could have been chewing on cardboard instead of Don Samuel's homemade *queso blanco*. Her stomach churned with the effort to digest the few bites she'd consumed.

"Someone spotted the body from the bridge," Simon added. "They reported him at a checkpoint by Sierra Verde. The soldiers retrieved him and now they're trying to get an identification."

"Such a sad end." Lupe took a sip of her coffee. "The way they lead their lives, they can't expect to die of old age."

Dora set down her drink. "At least they found the poor man."

"It's good Mr. Guerrero sent his daughter away." Lupe sniffed. "Copas isn't safe anymore."

Moni put down her fork. She'd been expecting Guerrero to go on a bloody rampage. Tearing up the area to find the killer. But nobody knew what happened to Paloma. In fact, gossip had her living in one city or another because Guerrero had been concerned with protecting his interests. For a horrible moment she wondered what had been done with her body. Was she buried in an unmarked grave somewhere? Had her father brought in a priest to speak over her, or told Paloma's mother? Could he really just wipe his own daughter's existence from the face of the earth in the name of protecting his interests?

She picked up her fork and pushed her food around the plate. She winced as she realized she was part of keeping Pablo's dirty laundry out of public view, whether she wanted to be or not.

"I wonder who killed him, and why." Dora's voice faded off.

"Him? What about the chief?" Lupe said, exasperated.

Dora shrank against the back of her chair. "I was just thinking out loud," she responded in a tiny voice.

"Either way, that man's life is nobody's business." Lupe raised her chin. "You don't need to be sticking your nose where it doesn't belong."

"*Mamá*." Simon's stern voice silenced the table. Lupe slouched in her chair, like a chastised child. So much for trying to play matchmaker between Simon and Dora this afternoon.

Moni tuned them out, pushing away the half-empty plate while Simon whispered to his mother. If this kept up she was going to lose the weight she'd gained back.

You filled in real nice. She could still feel Andres's hand moving over her body, his mouth exploring her intimately. Thoroughly. She frowned, grasping at a memory. *Thoroughly kissed.* That's what he'd said. She'd been too caught up in him to notice at the time. But honestly, that didn't sound like the cowboy she knew. She narrowed her eyes. Was there more to Andres Calderon?

Chapter Nine

Andres surged out of sleep, his senses alert and his shoulders tense. Something was wrong. He held his breath, straining to pick up any telltale clue of what woke him. His gaze shot from corner to corner, trying to see if anyone or anything sat in the murky darkness—waiting.

He slid out from under the covers, his feet slipping to the cold floor without making a sound. With one eye on the doorway, he backed up to the window and stuck a finger between the curtain and frame. Outside, everything looked normal, but the uneasy feeling pushed him to go find out for sure. Within seconds he'd pulled on dark jeans and jammed his feet into the nearest pair of boots. He grabbed the first shirt in the old-fashioned wardrobe on his way out.

Halfway to the door he stopped. Whatever might be out there blended into the surroundings, something he should try doing. He tossed the shirt onto a chair while he found another, dark enough to hide in the wardrobe's recesses.

His stomach rolled. This was really happening. He was heading into the night with only a well-honed pocketknife as a weapon. *God help me.* Two buttons were about all his stiff fingers could manage before stuffing the shirttails into his jeans then pulling his belt through the loops. He made his way to the hall with careful footsteps, then moved into the rest of the house. Everything was quiet, every corner empty.

He had to make sure the horses were safe. But how to go? Sneak over to the stable? Go directly or circle around the side? Either way, he would run a gauntlet. If a killer were outside, or there were more than one of them, he'd be armed. In the past few days, four people had gone to meet their maker. At least three of them didn't have defensive wounds, so they may not have it coming.

He turned the knob, tapping into his anger over feeling cornered to get him out the door. One step. Two. Each step felt like he was in the river, walking against the current. Even as he approached the stable, the building still seemed far away. The hair on the back of his neck stood on end. Fear could be a real bitch.

An image filled his head of Monica waiting by the fence the night they'd gone for Damian. She hadn't known who she was meeting, but she'd shown up anyway.

As he neared the stalls, bits of hay flew by. Uncle Rey's spirit was acting up again. The harsh wind carried an eerie whisper. Every shadow took the shape of a man. Right now he'd rather deal with a restless spirit than a dangerous predator.

The horses stuck out their heads, even Bailarina. He patted one nose after another, making sure to whisper a "Good boy" or "That's my girl" to each animal.

The tack room held no secrets so he checked the last little nook, where he'd sat with Monica at his feet. No varmints, animal or otherwise, but he couldn't shake the anxiety. He looked out toward the house on the hill, once his home. Everything seemed normal. The guys were on watch, one of them heading up from the bunkhouse like he had all the time in the world.

Should he go back? No. His grandfather had always believed in gut feelings. Right now, the old ways made a lot of sense.

Damian had left him his satellite phone. Should he call Monica to check on her?

The doctor's office sat at the edge of town, purposely set up so Guerrero's men could go in and out undetected. If he went, he could park behind the building and make his way around without disturbing anyone. The setup was great, unless you were a woman living there all alone—where no one could hear you if something went wrong.

He walked back to the house, still glancing into the shadows. After locking the door, he went to the kitchen and pulled the phone from where he'd hidden it inside a stack of plastic tumblers. His fingers tightened around the protective case. What if she was fine? He'd be waking her up and maybe worrying her. What would he tell her? *I had a bad dream, Doc. Wanted to make sure the boogie man hadn't gotten to you, too.*

Maybe he could go and look around quietly. It's not like he could get back to sleep if he was this wound up. Maybe finding out she was safe would settle this anxiety and let him get some rest. He grabbed his keys and hat then headed to town.

Monica awoke, trembling—her body overheated from a dream so vivid a whimper lodged in her throat. Andres Calderon—*again*. Shoulders bare, lips on hers, his cock sliding into her.

She had to get him out of her head. During the day, the girls and patients distracted her with chitchat. The long, lonely nights were a different matter.

The mattress held the heat she'd radiated, baking her neck, back, and bottom. She sat up, kicking off the Egyptian cotton tangled around her legs, then peeled off the stifling nightshirt, leaving her in skimpy satin and lace panties.

Turning, she stretched out on her stomach so the pedestal fan could cool her body and the spot where she'd been lying. *Dios mio*. Her breasts ached and her core yearned for the fullness she'd felt in the dream. The fan blew her hair across her back. She shivered, her skin hypersensitive. Why did she have to be so needy?

She bit her bottom lip. Her SAT phone sat in the other room. Damian had programmed his number in before handing it off. Andres would come...then so could she.

Their midnight ride still haunted her, sitting astride Rayo, touching from neck to ankle. *Ride my tongue like you rode against my cock*. She cupped her breasts. The sensation wasn't as satisfying as his touch would be. He worked on a ranch. The rope or reins or something left their mark on his hands. They were a working man's hands—distinct from every other male she'd been with—and all him.

He'd been the star of her fantasies and center of her thoughts way too often, since the moment she kissed him and he'd drawn her near. She was driving herself crazy.

The scuff of a boot against the sidewalk was faint, but enough to yank her from her fantasy. If someone needed medical attention they'd be sounding the buzzer. As seconds ticked by, the hair on her neck began to rise. She bolted off the bed, snatching up a cami and pulling it on as she stole through the darkness.

Avoiding the squeaky board in the hall, she glanced into the kitchen before slipping past. Carefully tugging her bag closer, she pulled out the nine millimeter Kris had given her. Taking a shaky breath, she released and double-checked the magazine as he'd taught her. Pulling back the slide, she winced at the loud snap. Did the noise filter downstairs? How the hell was she supposed to hear anything over her slamming heartbeat?

She grabbed the second magazine and realized she wouldn't have a place to hold it. *Damn.* Maybe those low budget movies had a point. A woman *would* go after the bad guy while wearing nothing but skimpy underwear.

She strained to pick up any sound. Silence. Maybe she was wrong—hopefully she was wrong. She grabbed her SAT phone, knowing she should call Kris to send help...but hit the number Damian programmed, instead. The line only rang once.

"Monica?" Andres's surprised whisper came across the line.

Her bare feet stole across the wooden floor. She positioned herself, back to the wall, between the door leading downstairs and the kitchen entrance. The flimsy lock captured her attention. Would someone be coming up? Could she really shoot if she had to? "You there?"

The urgency in his tone brought her back. Her hand tightened on the phone, and she swallowed down her fear. "I think someone's downstairs." Her whisper didn't have the calm edge she'd hoped, but her hands were steady. Kris's words came back to her, *Take your time and aim as if your life depended on it...because it will.* The scrape was closer this time. They'd be coming through the kitchen entrance.

"Fuck. It's me, babe."

She stopped mid-step, her weight balanced on the ball of her foot. Of all the idiotic things for him to do... "What is *wrong* with you? I could have shot you."

"I'm sorry," he whispered. "I was worried." His footsteps, no longer guarded, rang out on the last few steps of the outer staircase. She flipped on the safety and headed to the kitchen. After checking through the window she threw open the deadbolt, jiggled the knob, and stepped back. He came in, closing the door behind him while she set the weapon on the table, her hands shaking. She drew in a long, quivering breath and exhaled slowly, willing her heart to return to something that resembled normal.

"I woke up feeling like something was wrong."

Same as her. Only she wasn't about to share the details of her dream.

"I checked the house and the horses, then thought to check on you."

"Thank you." Most people were locking themselves in as soon as the sun went down. Would anyone have heard her if she'd been in trouble? "I...I woke up and heard a noise. I got dressed and came to get the gun...then I called you." *Because you've been running through my dreams.*

The strain of concern fell away from his features. His gaze moved down over her chest to where the ribboned seam rode low on her breasts. Her nipples contracted, pushing against the gauzy cotton with every shallow breath. "You sleep naked..."

The gruff statement sent her pulse pounding between her thighs. Heat blossomed low in her belly, recalling the images she'd pushed to the back of her mind—his hands on her hips, the evening breeze, her sliding forward in the saddle. *Dios*, could people really have sex that way? She swallowed hard, licking the edge of her bottom lip.

His hands caught her waist while hungry lips found hers, stealing her breath along with the remnants of her annoyance. She draped her arms around his shoulders, letting her chest press against the planes of his body. How many times had she fantasized about being tangled up with him? Finishing what they'd started in the exam room? But that day he'd been gentle, coaxing her closer, while tonight his kiss was hard and consuming, greedy to take everything she had to give. A shiver ran through her. Tonight, she'd give him anything he wanted.

She swayed against him, moving her hips from side to side. His palm slid down, burning through the lacy satin riding low on her hips. The calloused fingertips curled into the skin of her bottom, a welcome change to her experience thus far. The hard cock she'd been craving strained against her. Too high. She needed the pressure closer to the juncture of her thighs. Damn her genes for leaving her at a height disadvantage.

He pulled at the camisole, bringing the strap as far forward as it would come. Her nipple was still covered, but just barely. The turgid nub stood at attention, eager to cast off the bit of gauzy cotton stubbornly holding on. He cupped her, pushing her breast over the seam, freeing her sensitive tip to his touch.

A s her hips swayed against him, his hands moved of their own accord, seeking the silky skin he craved. Burying his face in her neck he breathed in her scent, delicate and utterly female.

It was hard to believe how well she fit against him, how natural and right they were together. Her ass drew his fingers and he willingly indulged, sliding over curves that felt tailor-made for him.

As his teeth raked lightly along her collarbone, it took everything he had to quell the urge to bite and suck, to leave his mark on her. Fortunately the delicate strap of her camisole offered a place to vent his alpha male urges. He tongued it into his mouth before clamping down and biting hard. A sense of satisfaction surged through him as he felt it snap. Releasing it, he returned to her mouth, swallowing her startled gasp. After kissing her into silence he lifted his head and leaned back.

Her nipple was still covered, but just barely. Cupping her breast, he tugged the fabric down, then moved his hand back up to squeeze and knead the soft flesh as she squirmed against him, every movement egging him on.

A jolt shot through her as a soft cry ripped from her, instantly snapping him out of his lust. As his gaze swept over her, it fell on her breast, the skin quivering and reddened where his fingers had been. He'd been careless with her. She wasn't a horse to be broken to saddle. She was a lady, unused to the work-roughened hands of a cowboy with no future living on the fringes of the cartel. What the hell was he thinking, drawing her into his life?

He leaned his forehead against hers, holding still while he struggled for composure and the will to do the right thing for once in his life.

"Tell me to go, Monica." His breath rushed out as he gripped her shoulders and gave her a slight shake. "Now."

"No." She leaned back to look at him, confusion written clearly on her face. It took everything he had not to buckle under the weight of those big eyes staring at him.

Gritting his teeth, he forced his fingers to let go of her. "It's better for you if I go." He took a deep breath, stepping back as his hands fell away and he turned to the door.

Her breath caught in her throat. Every cell in her body screamed. She was drowning in a tidal wave of lust, and he was walking away. Her chest tightened as she pulled up the camisole. She wouldn't beg. Pride wouldn't allow it. But she couldn't let him leave without a parting shot. "You were surprised I sleep naked. Well, I do. When I'm thinking of you." Jaw clenched, she forced the rest of the words out. "I should have just finish what I started."

Picking up the gun, she turned on her heel and left him at the door. Her fingers worked on their own, releasing the magazine and bullet she'd chambered while tears burned the back of her eyes and constricted her throat. She'd never be able to face him again without her cheeks burning with humiliation.

She set the gun in the backpack. Why hadn't she listened to her family and stayed the hell out of this backward little town? Life would have been so much easier if she'd never met—

Strong fingers clamped her arm, dragging her around. Her eyes went wide. Andres faced her, his features intense, his muscles tight, but his touch in firm control. "Do you have *any* idea how hard it is to walk away from you?"

She swallowed hard, tapping down the riot of emotions. "Then why?"

"Adrenaline's a bitch," he bit out. "I can't be gentle with you right now."

She cupped his cheek. "No one's asking you to."

"I...I don't want to hurt you."

Her pulse slammed at her core. "You won't," she assured him in a husky voice. "I started without you, remember?"

"Damn it, Monica," he croaked.

Anticipation bubbled within her. She drew closer, curling her fingers into the waistband of his jeans, brushing hidden skin, as she parted her lips ever so slightly. "I liked it."

His fingers dug into her hair a second before his lips crushed hers, pushing past to invade the recesses of her mouth. The hard angles of his body surged against her, whipping her senses into a frenzy. She meshed against him and matched every stroke of his tongue.

This is what she'd been missing. The feel of a rugged male, hungry for her. She slid her palms across his chest, enjoying the freedom to explore every ridge.

Fingers spread wide slid down the sheer material at her back, stopping at the curve of her ass. A moment later, he balanced her on the edge of the couch, supported by a hand at the base of her spine. She hooked a leg around his jean-clad thigh as he palmed her breast, brushing across her nipple, then under, to start again.

Desire pounded through her. She whimpered, arching into his touch. He pulled back, letting her catch her breath while his gaze trailed over her face. "Those sexy little sounds have been stuck in my head all day." Two fingers slipped the cami off her shoulder, unveiling her body then tracing the curve of her breast. "And I've been dying to taste the rest of you." His lips trailed after his hand to capture her nipple.

Wet heat surrounded the sensitive nub, demanding all her attention. With the first urgent tug, she was grasping at his shoulders. "*Dios mio*." She was trembling, lost in the way he nipped and suckled then swirled his tongue around the aching tip. Her eyelids drifted closed as her head dropped back. Sound vibrated along her throat, but she wasn't conscious of anything aside from a purr.

Why had she waited so long, denying them both? "I should have brought you upstairs—"

He cut her off with a quick kiss then shook his head. "It wasn't meant to be."

"Yet."

He nodded, then went back to nibble on her bottom lip. She slid her hand up to deal with his shirt buttons, eager for the hard planes they covered. But she hadn't counted on lust affecting her motor skills as her fingers fumbled with the small buttons. With little success on the one-handed endeavor, she moved down his chest to his belt.

He hooked his thumbs into the waistband of her panties, dragging them down to where her hips met the couch. Tingles of excitement danced along her spine as she wiggled off her perch to stand beside him.

He pulled her against him as he reached for her panties,

inadvertently stopping her progress on his zipper. They pulled apart in wordless agreement and switched in order to rid themselves of everything in the way. In the split second she took to pull the cami over her head, he'd opened his shirt—then stopped. His hands were on the belt, but his attention was on her body, sliding down to where he'd managed to get her underwear. "You're so fucking perfect." One quick jiggle of her knee and the scrap of satin lay at her feet. She stepped out of them, conscious of dampness covering her inner thighs.

The rasp of his zipper had her dragging in a deep breath. She pushed the dark shirt off his shoulders then looked down to where his jeans parted. His cock stood proud. Wide. Full. Ready. Her body responded with a flow of desire, anticipating the way he'd fill her. "Definitely should have brought you upstairs." Her fingers traced his length.

He chuckled deep in his chest. "We'll make sure you don't miss out this time." He pushed in to her hand. "As much as you can take." A needy little sound slipped from her, muffled against his shoulder.

His boots mocked her. They wouldn't come off without some work. *We'll never make it to the bedroom.* She'd barely managed the half dozen shaky steps as it was.

The couch sat within a few yards. What had he said when he was carrying her back to the office? *As much as I'd like to have your cute little ass in the air...*

She pulled away, taking dainty steps, letting him watch her. Hoping he'd be tempted to follow. She turned, tossing her hair off her shoulder, then sank slowly to her knees, bracing the front of her body against the couch, giving him his wish and hoping for hers.

"Monica..." Her name had never sounded so enticing. His steps echoed in the silence, drawing her nipples tight. A second later he dropped down behind her, his thumb doing a little circular motion as he made his way along her inner lips.

Her back arched, pushing out her hips, encouraging the intimate caress. Pleasure ramped up, turning into aching need. "Please." The word rode out on a shaky breath.

The belt buckle jingled behind her amid his mumbled, "Condom."

She shook her head, the tests at the clinic were thorough, he was healthy and safe. "Not necessary, and I'm on the pill."

He was still behind her for a moment, then fabric brushed against skin. Callused hands wrapped around her hips while the thick, hard tip pushed past her swollen lips, stretching her wide, filling her at long last. He kept going as her neck muscles forced her head back and her toes left the wooden floor. Denim finally pressed against her thighs. His hips were flush with hers. She'd never been so deliciously full.

A drawn-out groan filled the room. No description could have possibly done this moment justice. Even at the height of her lust-filled fantasies, she'd never come close to imagining something this good. "Andres. I need…" She was too wet to feel the sting of being stretched beyond what she'd ever experienced. Her body hummed with anticipation and need. *Move!* The word ricocheted in her brain, but she couldn't get the single syllable past her lips. She wiggled against him, hugging him inside her, spurring him on.

"Hold on, sweetheart." His first hard stroke drew her breasts across the couch's rough surface. A wave of pleasure raged through her body. It built up, pushed her closer to the edge as he continued to move. *No, not yet.* After spending so many nights dreaming of this moment, having it end so soon would be truly cruel. Control had never been an issue, but tonight she was struggling for breath, eager for the satisfying thrust of his hard cock.

"Is this what you need?"

She could barely manage a nod. But his fingers tightening on her hips warned that it wasn't enough.

"Tell me." His hips slowed, nearly bringing her to tears.

"Yes," she clamored. "I need you moving inside me." He rewarded her with added force. She reached out, dragging the cashmere throw to bunch at her cleavage. The two textures, harsh and buttery soft, fought for her attention each time she lunged forward. Stiff nipples reaped delight from the strange sensations, shooting sparks down to her clitoris. Broken sounds of pleasure accompanied every brush of denim against the sensitive skin of her inner thighs.

Her muscles tightened, sending a long-awaited orgasm crashing through her body with unexpected ferocity. She thrashed against him with an exquisite cry of release while Andres continued his hard ride. Her inner walls rippled, trying to hold on to him, precipitating the end. Finally he drove deep, and she was able to squeeze down as he emptied himself inside her.

Replete, she wilted on top of the cashmere throw, with Andres's arm coming down at her side. His heartbeat reverberated along her torso.

"You're okay?" His labored breathing echoed her own.

"Yes." *Way more than okay.*

He sat back on his heels, bringing her with him. The cushion dragged under her breasts, the lower curve making it past the edge until only the tips remained on the harsh material. She folded her arms, laying her forehead down.

They sat like that for endless minutes. Him covering her, except that part where her body surrounded him. Skin to skin. "I thought you were allergic to latex." A silly observation, but she was reasonably sure her brain had turned to mush.

His breath billowed on the center of her back, sending shivers down her spine. *Mmmm.*

"No."

Her brow furrowed. "But when you came into the clinic… you said 'no latex.'"

"I wanted your hands on me again." He nuzzled her shoulder.

She gave a satisfied smile, understanding his motive. Touching Andres had been her undoing. *Speaking of hands...* She took his left wrist, intent on enjoying his hand on her breast.

"Monica, stop." His palm squeezed shut, and he pulled back, releasing her.

She pushed up on her forearm. What happened? He'd gone from sated to tense.

"My hands are rough. I should have—"

Sitting back, she cupped his hand between hers, unfurling the long, tapered fingers. Her lips pressed against his palm, then she ran her cheek along the work-roughened skin.

"Don't do that."

She ignored the harsh whisper, loving the contrast in texture.

"I should've taken you up on your offer to give me something to help with the calluses."

The apology in his words tore at something inside her. He had scars, and they weren't all on his hands. Anger roiled in her chest. Someone had convinced him a woman wouldn't enjoy his touch. She'd happily throttle the idiot right now.

She rubbed her jaw along his thumb. "Your hands are honest; they reflect who you are." The changes in him suddenly made sense. How many times had she seen him withdraw when he was around others? She'd always thought it was just him and propriety, but this was much deeper. He perceived himself as a lower class than her—than most people. The question was why?

There was one sure way to make sure he knew it didn't matter to her. She managed a smile then took his free hand and ran it across her shoulder and neck with a light touch. Goose bumps erupted along her arms and torso. Could he feel her body's reaction? Would he know what he did to her? How she'd melted against him when he'd caressed her lower back the other night?

He cupped her right elbow, following the bumpy trail, discovering her body's response. She threaded her fingers through his then moved to her breasts, settling his palms against her hardening nipples. Seconds ticked by with both of them motionless. Her pulse jumped ahead. Too much? Too far? Too soon?

He pulled her flush against the heat of his chest, caressing her breasts, holding their weight. Her lids eased down. How long had she thought about this moment? "I've wanted you touching me, too," she confessed.

"I'm glad to hear that." He moved across her chest, pressing his forearm against one breast while cupping the other. "There's still a lot of you I'd like to touch." His free hand explored the curves of her body, over her hip, down her leg, before strumming up her inner thigh. Her insides fluttered with the riot of sensation.

His lips nibbled the back of her neck, dropping kisses along her jawline while his fingers discovered her hidden folds. Her body bucked with every pass. Awareness tingled across her chest, thighs, back, and up her neck to lash against the top of her head. "*Ah*."

In an instant, he obliterated the memory of every man who'd ever touched her. Damn, she was in trouble.

His cock pushed against her. "How about we move into your bedroom?"

R iding through hell had been worth it.

They lay in bed, barely a shared breath between them. Her full lips parted, letting him explore the sweet recesses of her mouth. A soft, firm breast filled his hand, the hard tip learning every hard ridge on his palm. He'd thought she'd at least complain. But the way she'd held him, run his hands over her body, she'd nearly undone him.

Delicate fingers stroked his cock, starting under his balls and ending with her thumb at the base of the head. She caressed him in the same rhythm her tongue played against his, seducing him from his exploration.

How much longer would he be able to keep this up? Every other heartbeat, her thighs tightened around the leg he'd insinuated between them. He wanted to touch and taste, to hear her enjoy the things he was doing. The urge to have her wrapped around his cock again was slowly taking over. He regretted his momentary hesitation when she'd told him he didn't need a condom. Monica would never lie to him, and thank mercy for that. He couldn't imagine not being skin to hot, luscious skin with this beautiful woman.

After a leisurely sweep under his swollen crown, her fingers curled around his, guiding his hand down to her ass. Her lips left him to trek across his shoulder and chest. This was a whole other layer of Dr. Monica Vasquez. He liked that she wasn't afraid or embarrassed about what she wanted.

His fingers came around her thigh, bringing her wet pussy to press against his leg. She gasped, nipping at his jaw. He chuckled. How had a woman so sensitive gone without sex for months? She was too damn tight to have been using a toy. "Show me what you were doing when I got here." He kissed her cheek, teasing at the corner of her mouth, squeezing the full curve of her ass.

"What?" Her breathless response was much like her deadly look. Slightly appalled, cushioned by a rich layer of interest. Enough to tighten his balls to a nearly unbearable level.

"I spent so many nights picturing you here." He teased

her lips, leading her on a chase, evading her until he was ready. "The sheet thrown aside. Hands on your breasts. Kneading. Sliding down your belly." He ran two fingers between her thighs, letting the pads stroke across her entrance, one at a time, before exploring further. "Your knees parting and your fingers buried here. Stroking. Spreading cream up to your clit."

Her hand slipped off his shoulder.

"Doing all the things I wanted to do." He licked her full lower lip. "Hearing you scream my name when you come."

She was breathless, rolling her hips to keep pressure against her most sensitive spots.

"While I was lying in bed at home, with my cock in my hand."

Clearly, the thought hadn't occurred to her. But the way her eyes fluttered and her lips parted with her ragged breathing…she was thinking about it now. He pulled away from her swollen folds, despite her whimper of protest, and brought her palm to her breast.

"Show me," he murmured again, laying her back against the sheets.

Her fingers curled around the mound, the thumb and index finger pulling at the darker skin, rolling the tip. The woman had haunted him during countless lonely nights.

"Both hands?" he encouraged with a hoarse whisper.

She moved her hand from under him, cupping the other breast, presenting the image he'd lost hours on. His cock grew incredibly full as he followed every move, every twist and tug.

"What did you picture me doing?"

"We-we were riding out together."

Yeah. She'd gotten payback for all the teasing. "Those damn buttons have been haunting me." The more he'd thought about her, the more he wanted her. He'd spent the next day nursing a raging hard-on. "If I'd done what I wanted…" He slipped kisses down her shoulder, his lips running over her soft skin. Her whimper brought him back to lap at the curve of her breast. The very spot his eyes had been glued to while they continued their search for Damian.

Inching across the delectable mound, he found the edge of puckered skin, nosing away the fingers holding her flesh so tight. He dropped kisses around the spot, returning for a taste.

Four sharp little nails tucked into his shoulder. He didn't have to check to know her eyes were on him. Maybe even edged with that killer look. Satisfaction filtered through every pore. His cock pressed against her, sending a shiver through his gut, pushing him closer to his limit. He didn't think he'd ever get enough of her.

The hard tip swayed with his tongue's first pass, returning expectantly for further attention. He was happy to oblige, with long licks and short dashes alongside the base. Lips parted, he settled over the tight bud, barely touching her skin, then inhaled through his mouth. Her sudden gasp pressed her firmly against his lips. He latched on, capturing her between tongue and teeth, sucking hard.

"*Annn-dres.*" Her body tightened, arching in response.

They rolled so she was on top, straddling him, freeing his hands to touch her. Soft jet-black hair slid across his shoulders like a whisper, enclosing him in a flowery-scented cocoon. She ran the back of her fingers down his face, then went on to caress his chest. Fuck. Every time he wanted to give her pleasure she turned it around on him. He tongued her cleavage, nuzzling the spot that teased him, before moving on to the other breast.

Reaching behind her, he cupped her ass, tightening on the firm mounds before exploring the smooth skin at the back of her thighs. Her hands moved along his shoulder and chest as her hips moved against him. Did she think he'd forgotten her screaming that she needed him moving inside her? Not likely.

His cock would rebel if he even thought about it.

Reaching down, he palmed the smooth skin of her thigh then followed up to where she sat astride him. The sudden hitch of her body pulled her nipple from his lips. He drank in the sight of her, pleasure washing over her features as his thumb played at her center.

Her lips parted. "Andres," she pleaded.

Satisfaction surged through him; her body responded to his slightest touch. He swallowed her surprised gasp, enjoying the taste of her. "We're not done here, sweetheart. In fact, we're missing the best part." He pulled her right hand down, threading his fingers over hers, then settled between her damp thighs, ignoring the protesting groan. "Is this…what you were…doing?" He dropped kisses at her pulse point.

"Uh-uh." Her voice vibrated against his lips.

"No?" He pressed her fingers into the wet folds. Pushing himself up on his elbow, he slipped his hand away to enjoy the view he'd arranged. Long hair pooled on the pillow, eyes closed, her left arm draped over his shoulder. One set of fingers dug into his hair, the other moved through her damp curls.

Too many nights and a vivid imagination had set up an array of images. There was little she could do that he hadn't already imagined and fantasized about. But none of it was as good as the real thing.

He gave her a long, leisurely lick across her breast while he nudged her thighs open then moved to kneel between her legs. His fingers trailed up to where she was pleasuring herself, moving along with her.

"Is this where you imagined my tongue?" His mouth watered at the thought.

"N-no." She shook her head. "You're inside me."

Mmmm. His cock was going to explode. "Like this?" Cupping her ass, he lifted her hips and pushed into her wet heat.

"Don't stop." The swollen folds gave way, welcoming him with a tight embrace. "Missionary." She shifted, letting him go deep. Wrapping her legs around his waist. "*Dios*. Th-this is better than—"

"Better than what, sweetheart?" Like his ego needed a boost. He was surrounded by her sweet pussy, her heels digging into the back of his thighs, while he watched her pleasure herself for his benefit.

"Dream. Woke up when you…"

Damn. His chest expanded, and his cock twitched. He fought the urge to drive into her. "Glad I didn't disappoint."

"God, no." She stopped, tightening around him, moving what little the position would allow. "*Knewwww.*" She exhaled. "You'd be good."

"Thought about it much?" He followed her hips down on the bed, going deep into her willing body.

Trembling hands reached out to his shoulders as he settled on top of her. "Once or twice. For inspiration."

He chuckled, rocking against her. The tension in her leg muscles increased. "Inspired to move fast and hard?"

Her expression froze. "I…um…"

Hadn't she spoken up before? Maybe she was used to a different pace. His balls were tight, needing an answer, *pronto*. As much as he didn't want to leave paradise, he pulled out, then drove in hard. "I can't hold on much longer. Yes or no?"

"Yes." Damn, he liked her voice all breathless. Eyes wide and interested, she braced her legs and shifted her hips up to cradle him.

He let go, gathering every bit of frustration, anticipation, and lust to make sure he met the little doctor's expectations. She'd have something new to think about when she snuggled in bed naked. Him. Them. The echo of their bodies coming together. Until he could be there with her for longer than a few stolen hours.

She tensed, ragged panting bouncing off his shoulder, and arched against him as she came. His pace slowed as he buried himself deeper, each thrust reaching farther into her core. Lowering his body, he closed his eyes, grinding his hips on hers, enjoying the way her pussy rippled on his cock until he exploded within her.

This moment would take him through a few nights—her damp forehead pressed to his neck, her hands grasping his back, the muffled panting against his shoulder, followed by a satisfied sigh.

He rolled, bringing her with him. Damn, he could easily die happy right now.

His gut fisted. He didn't know if it was because danger lurked or because it was trying to keep him from walking away from Monica.

"What's wrong?" She leaned away, following his gaze past the end of the shadowed hallway.

Getting out of bed he shook his head, having no ready answer. "This is gonna sound stupid, but I have a weird feeling." She eyed him without saying a word as he found his clothes. Each second of silence made him regret the statement.

"I'll go with you." She started pulling on her nightshirt.

"No." He wouldn't let her walk into danger with him. "Just give me a few minutes to look around." He stepped into the hall quietly, trying to keep ahead of her.

Swallowing hard, he glanced out at the shadowed apartment. A few cautious steps later, he stretched to check over the back of the loveseat. Nothing. To the right, the neat little kitchen offered a clear path to the far wall. Peering out the window, he saw her car sitting alone in the parking lot.

Instead of relief, his anxiety doubled.

The kitchen and living room didn't strike any alarms. But the doorway heading downstairs to the office pulsed with unseen danger. Fear dug into his back, like talons slowly ripping him open. Someone was down there.

Doc stood in the hallway to the bedroom, huddled in the shadows. He waved her back and motioned that he was going downstairs. He twisted the knob silently then pulled the door open a few inches, stopping when the hinges gave a tiny squeak of protest. Teeth clenched, he flattened himself against the doorframe and looked down.

Holding the door firmly in place, he squeezed through to the stairs, stepping down on every other one until he was at the foot of the reception area. That's when he knew. Whoever was here was by the entrance. Could it be someone needing the doctor? But then, why break in?

He crouched, setting his hand on the wall for balance as he took care to cross the narrow coffee area. At the edge of the hallway he stopped, closing his eyes and taking a deep breath to gather courage. Fists ready, he took a step. Two steps. A third.

His shoulders tightened until he wasn't sure he could move his arms. His pulse throbbed in his throat, and the hair on the base of his neck stood on end.

He registered an image just as his left shoulder hit the wall. He punched, hitting what felt like a concrete slab, but he pulled back and slammed his fist into the dark shadow again. The floor slipped out from under him. A second later he crashed onto his back.

His breath whooshed out, and his head buzzed, a series of images flashing before his eyes. A leather glove in place as a bull bucked. Rayo. Grandpa. Mom. Alex. Monica laughing. She wore the pretty white dress from the rodeo. Calm settled over him. He didn't care if he died, as long as he saved her.

He dragged in a breath while a bear of a man came into focus, looming over him. The steel band of a forearm dug across his upper chest while his other hand locked around Andres's throat in a death grip. "Where is she?" he growled.

Was this the killer? And what did he want with Monica? He'd expected someone would pull a trigger on him, but this man with the cold eyes would likely strangle him to death. The calm voice and deadly control made him fucking terrifying. No doubt he was the type who could tear through Guerrero's men and walk away from the massacre.

Blood rushed, leaving him lightheaded. Good God, Monica didn't stand a chance.

He stretched out his arm, hoping to get enough momentum for a punch to the liver. Then the light switched on. Confounded woman. What was she thinking? Anger fought fear, and his instincts kicked in. The bear looked up, and Andres aimed toward his face, but his fist ended up bouncing off a shrugged shoulder.

With few options left, he reached over, pushing his hand under his attacker's belt, and yanked down while trapping one of his legs. "Run, Monica! Run!" He held on to the leather strap, dragging in a breath as the guy's weight landed on him.

Hopefully the few seconds would give her a chance to escape.

"*Dios mio*," she cried. His blood went cold. She hadn't run. "Let him up!"

What? Andres dragged his face from under his attacker. The damn stubborn woman was down on one knee by the doorframe, tugging at the man.

"It's not me," the guy explained. "He's got me trapped." The weight over him shifted as he pushed himself up.

"Andres, please." She shuffled over, kneeling beside him. "It's okay."

He forced his hands to uncurl. Three knuckles popped as

he straightened his stiff fingers.

"Are you all right?" Her voice was sweet, coaxing him for an answer.

"I'm fine." He dragged in a breath, but his lungs couldn't seem to gather enough oxygen. "Just knocked the wind out of me." She helped him to the couch in her office, then turned.

"And you? What is this?" As angry as she sounded, she still threw herself in the guy's arms, holding him tight.

Andres jerked back. His chest collapsed inside him, igniting a fire that mushroomed up his body. Every muscle tensed. What the hell was happening? Just a few minutes ago Monica had been making love with him and now she was throwing herself into another guy's arms?

As Monica leaned back to look up at the giant, the man's gaze settled on Andres for a moment before looking down at her. His voice was low but carried far enough in the small apartment.

"We need to talk...alone."

Andres turned away, pushing the growing knot down his throat. "Don't let me stop you. I was just leaving."

Chapter Ten

As the town faded into the darkness behind him, he tried to reconcile the woman he'd been chasing with the one who watched him leave tonight. How could he have been so wrong about her? *Why didn't she just tell me there was someone else? I wouldn't have touched her…never gonna repeat that mistake.*

He shook his head. It just didn't fit. She hadn't given him a single come-on, he'd gone after her every single time, while she'd tried to act all professional. *She's a doctor and I'm wrangling horses for a living…*

His hands tightened on the wheel. He couldn't believe how wrong he'd been, again. In the end she was a cheat, just like Susana. He should just chalk it up to another lesson learned and be thankful he'd found out sooner rather than later.

What would keep a woman like her in a town like Copas anyway? All the exciting nightlife? He snorted.

He headed down the ranch road, not bothering to slow down or drive around the ruts. The truck leaned back and right. He slammed his heel onto the brakes, but not before the entire frame shook. *Fuck*. He had to focus. Guerrero hadn't had the sense to maintain the road in the years since he'd taken over.

Pulling off the road, he parked in front of his place, scattering a few of the ranch dogs. Better to avoid coming up on anyone. He'd take a quick look in the stable then get a pot of coffee on. A shower wouldn't hurt, but then he'd lose the light, flowery scent of her that still clung to him. Once it was gone, it would be an illusion. Just like her.

Wind blasted across the yard, carrying an eerie wail. He dug his chin into his chest and continued, letting his hat shield his face from the dust and bits of hay. The clang of a metal gate intensified as one of the bulls tried escaping into the pasture. The ranch hands should start milling around pretty soon. He'd tell Alex to have one of the guys go—

The unmistakable stench of smoke cut through his annoyance. His head shot up as a chill ran down his back. Rayo, Bailarina, and the other horses… He pushed forward, bolting across the uneven ground. The few yards to the building stretched out like miles. *Please, not the stable*.

In the sierra a fire could run through acres of scrub if left unchecked. The only place to remain relatively safe would be the main house. His mother had insisted on a quarter-mile clearance for a pool and garden that never came to be. The guards' endless footsteps had killed off any grass and plants long ago.

He careened into the stable, his heart slamming against his chest. His gaze ran across the stalls on either side. Wide-eyed horses snorted and bumped up against their enclosures. Thankfully, the danger wasn't around the animals.

He jogged through the stable, frowning as he got a clearer view out the open archway. In the distance, the house was outlined in the morning light. Only the sunrise was in the wrong spot. Fire. The house. The propane tank.

A flash of light, bright as the sun, erupted behind the house. The blast shattered the night, slamming him shoulder first into the ground. A fireball mushroomed over where the roof had been. Heat and debris rolled past him in slow motion.

Thoughts jumbled by the ringing in his ears, he staggered to his feet. The scene in front of him warped. Reeling from the blast, he stumbled, catching the doorframe until the world stopped moving.

Ranch hands poured out of their bunkhouse. Alex ran from his cabin's porch in a gray tank and worn jeans, his gaze riveted to the flames licking the sky.

The corner of the house buckled with a deafening crack as wooden beams and shingles collapsed into the living area. *No. No. No.* Even if he somehow succeeded in getting the ranch back, the house was gone. Numb, he tightened his hold on the weathered wood. Dad had built their home for Mom. She'd loved it, and now it was crumbling before his eyes. All the years together. The family. Holidays. They were gone, and nobody would ever be able to replace them.

Andres dragged in a breath, squeezing his eyes shut for a few seconds. What about the occupants? Dr. Treviño had his old room on the other side of the house, farthest from the explosion. He untangled his feet and forced them to move. One step. Two. Three. The next few were stronger but still unsteady. He followed the edge of the stable, needing the wall for support as long as possible before pushing himself off. Dr. Treviño, Lourdes, Maria, Susana and her son—all innocent bystanders in this situation. He had to see if they survived, then he'd check on Guerrero and the guards.

Got to get to the door. The path up to the main house hadn't ever seemed this steep. He trudged through a few more steps when a movement caught his attention. A deformed shadow took a wide path around the fire.

One of the dark-clothed guards materialized from the darkness, Pablo Guerrero leaning heavily on his shoulder. The older man favored his right leg. Somewhere along the way, he'd torn the sleeve of his pink shirt and lost a shoe.

Guess the old saying held true: only the good die young.

Dr. Treviño came up behind them, clutching his medical bag like a lifeline. *Thank God.* "Doctor. Are you all right?"

"Andres. *Hijo.*" Dr. Treviño reached out to steady him. "What happened to you?"

He took a deep breath. "Got knocked off my feet." They looked each other up and down. Andres gave him a crooked smile. The tank had exploded, the house was on fire, crashing down on him, and Dr. Treviño was dusty but impeccably dressed. His dark slacks were pristine, his belt in place, and his cuffs were buttoned tight. "I was coming to check on you."

The older man's arm tightened around him. "Carlo," he called out to Guerrero's newest goon. Carlo stopped halfway down the hill, swiveling with Guerrero still hanging off his side. "Wait."

"Take Pablo to Andres's cabin." He headed after them, glancing back over his shoulder at the chaos they'd escaped.

Andres followed the group, his stomach roiling with every step. Alex rushed over with Susana beside him, cradling her screaming child. She hesitated, but Alex pulled open the screen door and pressed her forward, following her into Andres's home.

"Alex." Dr. Treviño settled into the couch. "What's the status?"

"The house is gone." Alex shook his head. "Nobody else made it out." He hesitated a moment, shooting a covert glance at Guerrero. Clearing his throat, he stared down at the floor. "The fire pond wasn't kept up, neither was the equipment. Without them there's nothing we can do except let it burn out, hope it doesn't spread."

Fear mushroomed within the group like a tangible thing, filling every corner. Nobody said a word, but the child's incessant crying served to strain already frayed nerves. Susana stepped into the kitchen doorway, humming a tune in an effort to calm her son.

Dr. Treviño cleared his throat. "Get the other guards," he ordered. "They should give us some answers."

"I didn't see them among the men." Nobody had to say the words on everyone's mind. If they were around back, they might not find enough of them to recognize.

"Check the bunkhouses." The screen door slammed closed behind Alex.

Andres started for the door. "I'm going out there." His childhood home was burning to the ground and all he could do was watch the ranch hands chasing stray embers.

"No, muchacho," the doctor chastised, rubbing his right wrist. Andres stopped at the door. "Alex is right, there's nothing anyone can do to save the house. Don't get yourself hurt, or worse, when you'll still have to rebuild."

There was nothing left. The firebreak would keep the blaze contained, but nothing within fifty miles would put out that inferno. Another loud crack and a wall went down. He turned back to the room, unable to watch.

"You're lucky you don't have a concussion." Dr. Treviño looked to Susana. "We found him heading to the house. He'd been knocked senseless by the blast, and he was still trying to save *me*."

Andres shifted, uncomfortable with the change in conversation. "I'm just glad you made it out safely."

"Thank you. I've been in shock since I found Carlo coming out of the house with Pablo in tow. I'd checked the bedroom, but didn't find him."

"He fell asleep in the front room, watching television." Carlo turned to Guerrero, who was huddled into an overstuffed chair, for either praise or confirmation. Neither was forthcoming. "I had guard duty along that side of the house. I saw him crashed out every time I walked past the window."

Pablo Guerrero looked dazed. He'd been in a drunken stupor since Paloma. Even a drug lord could fall apart if he lost a child.

"We'd had such a nice dinner last night," Dr. Treviño said wistfully. "I helped Lourdes prepare her famous bread pudding for everyone at the party. Did you have some, Pablo?"

"A few bites."

"You, Carlo?"

"Nah." He folded his massive arms. "Too much sugar."

Dr. Treviño's shoulders deflated. His pale face held more years than they did a few weeks back.

Andres glared at Carlo. Idiot. Didn't he realize Dr. Treviño was trying to lighten the mood? Maybe get some conversation started to break the stranglehold on everyone's nerves.

Susana shifted the baby to her other arm, trying to soothe him. Andres crossed his arms and turned his attention to the wall. Anything was better than looking at her.

A picture commanded his attention, his parents standing proudly in front of a prize stallion his father had purchased years ago. Once upon a time he had thought that someday he would be in a picture like that. Then Susana had come into his life. Based on a single lie he had believed like the sucker he was, he'd made one bad decision after another. Monica could have been the woman who changed that, but now it looked like she was just the latest in his string of poor choices. Maybe the fire was a sign that it was time to let go of his dreams once and for all.

He sighed and glanced around, finding Susana's attention on him. He met her gaze straight on. Once again she looked him up and down, only this time her assessment changed. Her hips swayed slowly side to side as she rubbed the baby's back. She lowered her head slightly while still watching him, a move he once found seductive. Now it looked cheap and grasping. He could almost see her calculating his value. Whatever she might have once been was gone, the illusion stripped away in the rush to find her next sugar daddy. She was, in a word, pathetic, and regardless of where his life was, it would always be better than hers.

He took a deep breath, blew it out, and felt the resentment trickle away. He could never like her again, but he could pity her, and it was the only fitting thing left to do at this point.

Rapid footfalls grew louder. Andres turned toward the door. Alex huffed as he pulled open the screen, standing alone. He opened his mouth, but apparently the sight of Susana stopped him. Instead, he shoved a baby bag at her then gave Dr. Treviño a sharp nod. The man struggled off the couch, leading Andres and Carlo outside.

"What happened?" Their three voices layered over one another.

Alex shifted his weight, his face pale. "The guards for the day shift were in the bunkhouse. Dead. All four had their throats slit."

Silence fell over the group. Each man absorbing the news in his own way. Susana joined them, still struggling with the crying child. "Mr. Guerrero was getting agitated with us," she explained.

Carlo squinted, studying the surroundings through the chaos. "They're out to get us all."

"Who?" Susana tightened her hold on the baby.

Andres wondered the same thing. The murderer was a ghost. He'd added four hired killers to his list of victims. If not for the bodies, he might have thought the explosion was an accident. But there was no mistaking this for anything other than calculated, cold-blooded murder. Andres looked up to find Carlo staring at him. "Why were you out sneaking 'round?"

Andres jerked back, struck with a sudden dread. He shook his head, aware of where this conversation could go. "I wasn't sneaking around."

"Wait a moment," Dr. Treviño protested.

"No. He just got here. I saw him from the porch," Alex supplied, much to Andres's surprise. Carlo's suspicion he understood, but Alex?

"You were out the night Paloma was killed, too," Carlo added with conviction. "You didn't come back all night."

Susana stepped back, looking at him with accusatory eyes.

Wrong. Carlo was off on the night in question. He'd helped get Damian out the night *after* he'd discovered Paloma's body. Both then and tonight he'd been with Monica. Would she be willing to confirm they were together? Would he even be given a chance to provide an alibi?

"This is ridiculous." Dr. Treviño scoffed. "I saw the boy leave last night, and Alex saw him arrive. Besides, he was heading to the house, not away."

Carlo smoothed his slicked-back hair, at a loss for words. He looked from one man to the other, knowing he had no support. "You mark my words, someone's out to get every one of us." He set his jaw, trying to jut out his slanted chin.

Susana shifted the baby again. "Ah. Why me?" she whined at the guard. "I just got here and I have nothing to do with Mr. Guerrero."

"Neither did the cop." Carlo narrowed his eyes at him. "But someone took *him* out, too."

"Carlo," Dr. Treviño interrupted. "Go collect Pablo and bring him out to the truck. We must go, it is no longer safe here for him."

Andres stood in stunned silence.

Susana backpedaled before turning to follow Carlo to the

house. He'd seen that calculating look on her face before. He wished he could feel sorry for the guy, but he'd just accused him of murder. Somehow it seemed they both got what they deserved.

"You're leaving?" A thick lump settled in his throat.

"Let's go inside." Dr. Treviño led them into the stable, looking around at the chipped paint on the wooden planks. "While I'm sad to leave this place, it's time you had your home back. I know how much Rancho del Sol means to you and that you'll do right by the Calderons."

Andres drew a deep breath. It couldn't be this easy. "What if he decides he doesn't want to leave?"

Dr. Treviño slid an arm around his shoulder and lowered his voice. "Would you stay at the place your daughter had been murdered, especially in such a fashion? He is a very ill man, and cannot get better here, haunted by memories. You understand."

Andres nodded, still dazed. Thoughts crowded his mind. What about all his other patients? Monica wasn't going to stay. Her time in Copas had always been temporary. She had a life to return to. He'd witnessed the love she had for the guy with his own eyes. But that didn't matter. None of it mattered. He had his heritage back. So why did it feel so hollow now?

"Thank you," he said hoarsely. "I can't express...but where will you go?"

"I'm taking him down to the coast. He mentioned having a beachside property he hasn't visited in years." The doctor squeezed his shoulder, his features softer, like a weight had been lifted off his shoulders. "I'll ask you not to share that information."

"Of course." The enormity of the situation took a full second to filter through his brain. The doctor had just given him the biggest gift he'd ever received. Freedom. There was nothing he could do to stop the grin spreading across his face. He turned to Alex, expecting the same pleasure or at least relief at the news. Instead, his friend's smile was tight. Andres's joy dissipated. "You're going, too?"

"Yeah." He shifted his weight to one hip. "I guess I'll stick with the doctor for a while longer. I've got some stuff to figure out before I can decide what to do."

Even with everything that had gone wrong with their friendship, he couldn't imagine the ranch without Alex. They'd spent most of their lives running around together, exploring every cave on the property. Andres had made life-changing decisions based on Susana's lies. Coming between Alex and Susana, however unaware he had been, had driven a permanent wedge between the two men.

He turned to Dr. Treviño. "Would you mind if I talk to Alex privately?"

"Go right ahead." He took a few steps away.

Andres tipped his head toward the other end of the stable. Every step tightened his gut a little more. Alex took them out the other door. A couple of dogs followed at their heels. He waited until they were clear of the building to reach for a nine millimeter from his back. "I grabbed this off a night table, thinking you might need it."

"Thanks, bro." Andres took the weapon, checking the magazine and safety before sticking the barrel into the back of his belt. Even with all the shit between them, Alex still looked out for him. How did a guy start a conversation about how big of an ass he'd been? "Hey. You don't have to go." Tension rolled off Alex in a thick wave. "I may not be able to pay you what you're making now, but you'll have a roof over your head."

Alex shifted his weight, looking out across the property. Could he be thinking about the work it would take to get the ranch going again? An extra pair of hands would be welcome, but his reason for wanting Alex around went beyond help.

They were family, even though they didn't share the same blood.

"Shit." Andres slapped his hand against his thigh. "I'm doing this all wrong." His breath rushed out. "Man, I'm sorry." He shook his head, not knowing how else to approach the subject. "About everything. I never should have believed Susana over you." Alex's features lost all emotion. Good or bad, he should get the words out. Tell him the truth and admit how wrong he'd been.

"I didn't love her." He wet the corner of his lips, his mouth suddenly dry. "Not like you did." His heart pounded, more for the grief his friend had endured than for the woman who'd come between them. Truth be told, he hadn't known what love was until recently. Until Monica blew into his life with her long black hair and fiery determination.

"I got tangled up in wanting to…save her. And I couldn't see what was going on around me." Alex remained silent, like he had back then. He should have spoken up, told him the score. "Why didn't you tell me you two were together? If I'd known, I never would have gotten involved with her to begin with."

Alex rubbed his hand along the back of his neck. His mouth flattened into a grim line. "You were home from college. You had a degree, and a future in front of you." He finally looked him in the eye. "You could have given her a hell of a lot more than I ever could. And the truth is…maybe… looking back, I'm not sure I ever really loved her, either."

Andres wondered if Susana had jumped a sinking ship. He'd just been stupid enough to ignore his parents' warning. Only after everything had gone wrong had Lourdes told him about Susana having dated Alex…

"Still, I didn't expect you to be such a bastard." Alex's face twisted with anger and disappointment. "How could you leave her over there? She was all alone and pregnant in a country where she didn't know anybody else."

Andres met Alex's gaze. It was past time to be honest and stop playing hero...and martyr. He'd screwed up, and it was time to own it. Andres cleared his throat. "I didn't leave her, she left me. She told me the kid wasn't mine and just like that"—he snapped his fingers—"she was gone." He took a deep breath. "I'm not gonna lie, I wasn't sorry it ended, I just wasn't happy about having to slink back home like a dog with his tail between his legs.

"I was pissed, but to tell the truth, bro, I was mostly goddamned embarrassed. Still am." His gaze returned to Alex. "I can tell you how sorry I am from now till hell freezes over...and I know it doesn't excuse anything. I just want another chance." He glanced at the smoldering remains of his family home. He swiped a hand over his face. "I'm not sure that's even possible now."

Alex nodded, his expression turning thoughtful. Andres had to ask. "Did she tell you the baby was mine?" Alex frowned. "No, Dr. Treviño told me. I figured it was true, because he kept going on and on about family and sacrifice."

It made sense. Dr. Treviño had given him a similar talk. But at the time he'd thought he meant Susana and the sacrifices she'd have to make as a single mother. "It's not. We hadn't been around each other until yesterday."

Alex blew out a breath. "She asked me to drop her off in town with the money Dr. Treviño sent. When I said no she got pissed and got out of the truck." He spit, turning back with a scowl. "Now that I know she's not your baby mama, I can tell you I found her at my place when I got back. She tried a different tactic to get the money I'd been given to go shopping." Alex shoved his hands in the back pockets of his jeans and kicked at a dirt clod. "I'm sorry about the crap she put you through, brother. Once you were gone there was no denying she was only with me to get to you. Guess that's where my pride kicked in and kept me from owning up."

Andres released a long slow breath. A knot of tension he'd had sitting in his chest finally released. "Now it looks like she's going for Carlo."

Alex sobered. "And that guy's stupid enough to fall for it."

One dog growled then another joined in. In the stable, Dr. Treviño was milling about. Andres frowned. Who was he talking to? Rayo? He shook his head. Trust the doctor to make a crazy moment look dignified. The damn horse was probably giving him lip for standing there without grabbing a brush and making himself useful.

A shadow fell across the far entrance as the wind picked up. Andres's shoulders stiffened. "You bastard." Carlo's voice rang out as he stared at them through the stable. " — his kid?" Half his words were drowned out by a sudden gust and the dogs' wailing.

"**N**ot all of them died, *doc-tor*." Carlo stood at the doorway, seething.

Medical training ingrained the need to avoid emotional involvement during a crisis. Reynaldo Treviño thought he'd mastered the skill years ago, so it surprised him when his pulse kicked up as Carlo interrupted him saying good-bye at the memorial for Rey Calderon. The father he'd never known. Over the past few months he'd imagined being caught working against Guerrero. Mostly he'd expected the cold finger of fear at his neck, but he was clearheaded, his muscles tensing as he waited for Carlo to act.

In the split second it took for the gun to travel from Carlo's waistband to point the massive barrel in his direction, time slowed to a crawl. Dispassionately he noted the barrel seemed larger now that he was staring down it. His gaze fixed on it. The bullet would rip through his flesh, muscle, and organs, maybe ricochet and cause additional damage. If it was a hollow point...

The wind whooshed in behind him, picking up dirt and debris in its wake. Carlo's hateful glare disappeared with the dense cloud hitting him full force. Blinded, he pulled the trigger, sending the bullet on a wild trajectory.

Gunfire erupted around him, echoing from both sides of the building. Somewhere behind him Alex and Andres were yelling. A burning lash sliced along his external oblique muscle, sending him crashing against the wooden planks. Horses screamed in terror, high-pitched squeals punctuated by hooves pounding against the unyielding wooden enclosure. The resulting shock waves reverberated along his wrist and shoulder.

When Reynaldo opened his eyes the dust cloud had cleared. Carlo blinked incessantly, looking down at the splotches staining his dark shirt. He stumbled, and his finger tightened on the trigger, sending a bullet into the doorframe, earning himself another shower of gunfire from the doorway behind him. The most skilled trauma surgeon would not be able to repair the damage in time. Carlo's limp body hit the ground with a deep, resounding thud.

Boots pounded against the earth. "Doctor." Andres's eyes, so dear to him, were wide and concerned. "You're bleeding."

"We'll get you to town," Alex assured him.

"Yeah." Andres pushed at his side, putting pressure on the wound. "Monica will fix you right up."

"Let me see," he rasped, needing to gauge the extent of his wound. Andres pulled the shirt away to rip the material apart. "This is barely a scratch. Adrenaline will keep the pain at bay for a little longer." He dragged in a breath. "I need to get Pablo away from here immediately." He leaned in, putting pressure against the wound. "He's been so distraught I had to administer sedatives so he'd rest." If everything had worked correctly, Pablo would have been sedated during the explosion, and they could have avoided all of this.

Both men nodded their understanding. "I'd rather we be on our way as soon as possible." He pointed to Carlo's prone body. "Check on Carlo and get me my bag." Alex scrambled to kick away the gun before he squatted to check the body. Straightening, he shook his head then disappeared around the wall.

"Andres, *hijo*. You need to do right by your family." He couldn't possibly understand what it was like to grow up without a father. And he'd do everything in his power to make sure that didn't happen to another Calderon.

Andres's jaw tightened. "Susana's child isn't mine, Dr. Treviño." He shook his head. "I just found out she led you on."

Reynaldo stared, dumbfounded. It hadn't occurred to him that the woman would have lied. He expected the woman Andres chose to have integrity. That's why he'd tried to get her and the child out of harm's way, sending them to Monterrey while he dealt with Pablo Guerrero.

If only Carlo had eaten dessert, he would have wiped out all vestiges of the cartel with the fiery blaze. Granted, he hadn't had time to account for all possibilities. Not when Lourdes had discovered evidence that would have implicated him in Paloma's death. There'd been so much blood. Some of it was bound to end up on his clothing.

"I think she'd gotten to Carlo, too," Andres continued. "I heard him yelling about the kid." His voice broke. "I'm so sorry you got caught in the middle. He must not have seen you standing there when he came after me."

Reynaldo squeezed his hand. The poor boy thought he'd been shot by accident. No, Carlo had just come upon him at an inopportune moment. Well, no matter. He could still take Pablo away and figure out what to do with him.

"I'll be fine." He managed a weak smile as he straightened himself. "You go take care of what you need to do." Andres hesitated. "Go on, I'll wait here for Alex."

He nodded once, then stalked off toward the house.

It was over, for the time being. He slumped against the wall, holding the tattered shirt against his wound as adrenaline worked through his body. His gaze lifted to the framed picture of Reynaldo Calderon which hung over the corner of the doorway. "*Papá*, your home is back within the family, as I'd promised."

"A y-ay-ay," Lupe screeched as she braced herself on the dashboard.

"We're almost there." Monica reassured her frightened companion while maneuvering around the lake-sized craters in the road. They'd called an unspoken truce while loading the car with supplies.

For months Monica had been anticipating the job in emergency medicine. But as she handed Simon a bin of gauze, antiseptic, and gloves, she'd realized she'd found a sense of community, and maybe family, that she'd never felt in the city.

By the time they were packed, the line of helpers reached the front door. Dora agreed to stay behind, with Simon checking in on her. They'd shared anxious hugs and pleas to be careful before taking off. Dora and Simon watched from amid the crowd, her hand held tightly in his. Lupe had been too busy staring into the distance to pay any attention.

They were getting closer to the smoke—and Rancho del Sol.

Monica's stomach roiled. *Andres*. Had he made it home?

Was he safe? He hadn't answered her call. Was the phone turned off? Was he at the scene of the explosion...or a part of it? She had seen his face when he left and could imagine what he was thinking.

He'd all but stomped out the door, and she'd let him. But Kris had a bounty on his head, and she wouldn't expose him, not even for Andres. Kris had waited, watching the scene with his arms crossed and eyebrows raised, silently demanding an explanation.

While she had refused to give him one, she knew it was obvious Andres was her lover. After assuring Kris she was fine, the situation was fine, the whole damn world was fine, she'd tried shoving him out the door.

He'd come with the intention of taking her home. He wouldn't risk losing her to the cartel, the way he'd lost his parents. The chief was dead, Paloma was dead, they had no police force, and now something was up at Rancho del Sol.

She was in the middle of trying to get answers when the low rumble of the explosion brought her to a screeching halt.

In the distance, the flames reached above the trees. Just as she'd feared, Andres's ranch. The main house was on fire. Her throat constricted with unshed tears. *Dios, please let him be safe...* He didn't live there...did he? Dr. Treviño did. She hit the gas, earning a few expletives from Lupe as they sped off the main road and up the drive.

The car shuddered, ending with another hard clank from somewhere beneath the vehicle. *I can't deal with you right now.* With the last bit of momentum, she pulled off the driveway, throwing the gearshift into park before pushing the door open. The seatbelt jerked her back against the seat. "Ahhhh. Stupid...damn...belt."

She fought with the release while Lupe waddled on ahead. *Please let him be okay.* She grabbed her medical bag out of the back and flung the door closed.

The front of the once beautiful home was barely recognizable. Part of the hand-carved porch swing she'd admired during her last visit lay on the hood of an SUV, charred and broken.

Thankfully, only a couple of trees grew next to the house so the blaze was contained. Men in various states of dress were spread around the grounds, putting out small brushfires. None of them Andres. She'd pick out his form in a heartbeat.

The only person she did recognize was Alex, who ducked his head and plowed on. Should she go ask questions, find out what happened? Fear choked her, leading her mind to the worst-case scenario. She needed answers as badly as she needed her next breath. *Andres...*

Just then the screen door to a lone cabin opened and a woman stepped out, catching her heel on the threshold. Moni's hand tightened on the strap of the backpack as she watched Andres step quickly to her side, his arm curled protectively around the woman's waist, steadying her and the wailing bundle she held to her shoulder. In his other hand, he clutched a light blue bag with a baby bottle sticking out a side pocket. It could be nobody but Susana...with a baby.

Moni's heart stuttered as Andres bent his head to Susana's ear and said something to her. She nodded, and they continued down the porch. Even disheveled the brunette was pretty, not beautiful in the classic sense, but slender and delicate right down to her dainty ankles.

"Oh damn," Lupe muttered, incredulous.

Moni's steps slowed. She straightened until her spine was painfully stiff then retreated into herself as the couple and their baby hurried past her toward his truck. She watched while Andres pulled open the passenger door, carefully taking the baby in his arms while the woman climbed in. Moni's gaze locked onto his face as he looked down at the child. She saw the slight crease in his forehead, the tender way he tugged the blanket up around the face, shielding it from the smoke. Every gesture tore at her. He would be a good father. The woman murmured something, and he looked up, hesitating a moment before handing her the bag and then the baby. He closed the door carefully, pushing it tight against the truck rather than slamming it shut. Finally he turned and looked at her. His face was carved from stone, and the eyes that had danced with humor and glinted with lust were now distant and remote. Anguish lashed every cell of her being, but she held strong. This couldn't be happening, yet the hard lines around his mouth dug deeper as he stared at her. She opened her mouth, but he shook his head. He dropped his gaze and stepped around the front of his truck, as if she wasn't standing right there in front of him.

"Andres?" She hesitated. What could she say?

"Not now." His back and shoulders stiff, he continued around to the driver's door.

Tears burned in her eyes, but they wouldn't fall. The truck pulled away, and Lupe came up to her. "I can't believe nobody told me they had a baby. What did you say to him?"

Yeah, you and me both. Moni fought against the pain of betrayal and loss closing in on her like a tsunami. How could she have fallen for his lie? *We're not together…* Yet here they were, leaving his home — together. With their child. She was acutely aware that Lupe was waiting for an answer.

"I asked if the baby was injured. He said no." The lie came easily though her words were thick and pained.

Lupe sniffed beside her. "And he would know this how? He should have let you examine it."

Monica mustered up a shrug. As smoke billowed over them she waved her hand in front of her face and coughed. "We need to get away from this. Over there." She gestured toward the stables. At least this time she had an ironclad excuse for reddened eyes and tears. This time nobody would know how much it hurt inside.

"I was right," Lupe stated with assurance. "No wonder her parents wouldn't have her."

Was that part of his initial reluctance last night? Knowing he had a woman and child at home waiting for him? Swallowing hard, she called herself every kind of idiot. She should have listened when he told her to send him away.

"Over here." Lupe rushed ahead to the SUV parked by the stable. "Doctor!"

Moni forced her feet to move. She trudged behind Lupe, arriving just as Alex opened the rear doors of the SUV then seated Dr. Treviño and his bag. "Go," he said to Alex. "Take care of what you need to, then get Pablo." Some unspoken message passed between them.

Moni moved to stand beside her mentor, immediately focusing on the blood at his side. Dropping her bag she reached for the zippers while pummeling emotions into the hollow where her heart sat just minutes ago. She couldn't seem to find anything, regardless of how many zippers she opened.

"I'm fine, dear." His calm tone did nothing to reassure her, but she was fine if he believed her nerves were for him. "I just need you to bandage me up." He handed her gloves out of his bag, holding on to them for an extra second when she'd tried to accept them.

She met his eyes.

"This is nothing," he said with finality. The message came through loud and clear.

She was to bandage him up and keep her mouth shut.

Behind her, the nurse paced behind the vehicle.

"You shouldn't have driven here by yourselves," Dr. Treviño murmured. "It's too dangerous to have women out alone."

"We had to come," Lupe said adamantly. "I'm sure the

whole town is concerned, knowing you're here…with these people." She ended in a harsh whisper.

Bandaging done, Moni administered a shot to help with the pain, then helped move him to the backseat on the driver's side.

Alex opened the far door, maneuvering Pablo Guerrero into the vehicle. The older man slumped into the corner, a blood-stained bandage covering his leg. Pink would have seemed an unlikely selection for his shirt, if she didn't know about Paloma and her fondness for the color. The vacant eyes and heavy jowls dragging down his jaw attested to the hell he'd been through lately.

Monica frowned and leaned in, peering closer at Guerrero's eyes. She dug into her side pocket and pulled out a tiny flashlight. With a quick flick of her wrist she aimed the beam at him for a second, then moved it away. His pupils were pinned and nonreactive, and he didn't even glance her way as she straightened up. He wasn't drunk, he was stoned out of his mind on narcotics.

Clicking off the light, she shook her head. She couldn't muster up too much surprise that a drug kingpin might succumb to the very poison with which he'd made his fortune. At least it had kept the man from rampaging across the countryside seeking revenge.

"Monica, I'm sorry to have put you through this." She snapped her attention back to Dr. Treviño, nodding an automatic response to his apology. "I never expected things to progress this far."

The disaster around them or the disaster her life had turned into? Tears pricked at the corners of her eyes, overflowing down her cheeks. Refusing to break down in front of her mentor, she blinked in rapid succession, trying to stem the tide to no avail.

He placed a hand over hers. "Go home, Dr. Vasquez.

There's nothing more you can do here." Something shrank in her chest, agreeing with the stark truth of his statement.

R eynaldo relaxed against the passenger door. The shot Monica gave him numbed the pain and left him lethargic.

"You okay over there, Dr. Treviño?" Alex looked back at him through the rearview mirror.

"Mmmm." Reynaldo nodded as they merged onto the highway and Alex sped up. "I was just thinking…"

"About?"

"Copas has roots." He looked out at the fence posts running past them. They were melding into one column then separating again. "The people *care*." He sniffed, his eyes burning. "My mother cared. She-she was a good woman. A lady."

Alex tilted his head. "She was from here?"

Reynaldo shifted forward, his chin hitting his chest. He tried lifting his head but for some reason, his neck refused to perform the simple movement. "The family moved to Galala-Gadala…Gua-da-la-ja-ra." He chuckled, adjusting in his seat. "They moved so moth-her could go to school." Alex nodded. "Ed'cation is important."

"Yes, it is." Alex agreed.

"I would have been happy." Sorrow weighed him down. "A happy little boy." But she went to school. *School*. And he went to school. A doctor. He smiled, remembering the joy of teaching others. Those special few… "Monica cares." Deep breathing echoed against the glass. "I thought she'd be good for Andres." He settled back, lulled by the hum of tires on pavement.

How many hours had he spent with eyes so similar to Andres's staring back at him? The old photograph had been put away, meant to be kept from prying eyes. But a curious little boy was apt to find hidden secrets then fit the pieces together.

Family had brought him to Copas. The family his grandparents had robbed him of when they'd found out his unwed mother was expecting. Now, for Andres's sake, his nephew and papá's only blood relative still on the ranch, he was leaving—and taking the garbage with him.

Chapter Eleven

Monica sat at the foot of the bed, her eyes fixed on the luggage she'd prepared for her return home. She should have been on the road an hour ago, but the day's events still held her attention in a stranglehold.

Guerrero had stirred up the devil himself. Whoever was out to get him could blend in so well nobody realized he was there. He'd managed the impossible, clearing out the cartel from the area in one final blow. Andres would get his property back, and the town would have a better chance of getting another doctor. Someone who didn't want to skulk away again, to lick a new set of wounds. Tears clouded her vision, and she dropped her forehead into her palms, angry at the loss she couldn't seem to smother.

The door leading down to the office opened a few inches with a protesting creak. Wide-eyed, she jerked up, her gaze going to where she normally left her backpack. She cursed under her breath when she saw the empty spot. The door opened wide, letting a familiar form into the apartment.

"You okay?" Kris advanced toward her with a concerned

frown.

"I'm fine." She slouched, letting the tension ride out of her back. "You heard about the ranch?"

"Yeah. And you're not answering your damn phone."

She winced, realizing he'd probably thought the worst when she hadn't answered her phone. "I'm sorry." She shot off the bed, wrapping her arms around him as he hugged her back just as hard. "I didn't realize I left my bag in the car." Proof she'd been in shock since she left the ranch.

"You had me worried." Kris's bear hug loosened. He pulled away, holding her at arm's length as he chastised her. "When I got word the explosion was at the ranch, I called you. You didn't answer." With the dark hair and annoyed twist of his mouth, he reminded her of her father.

"Oh God." He'd been worried about the chatter at Rancho del Sol enough to jump on a plane and head down to pull her out, but of course she hadn't listened. "I'm soooo sorry. I…"

He kissed the top of her head. "As long as you're alive, I'll get over it." She pulled away, immediately missing the support.

"We went to the site but were ushered out pretty quickly." She swallowed the lump in her throat at the reminder of Andres. "Nobody needed medical attention."

"No survivors?" he asked, with little emotion in his voice.

"I can confirm Guerrero and Dr. Treviño made it out of the house alive." She still didn't know the full extent of the damage or the lives the killer had claimed.

"We had another agent on the inside. He hasn't checked in."

This part of the job she could do without. There was no easy way to handle a notification. At least Kris would be expecting her words. "I didn't see any of the security crew." Silence stretched out. She didn't prod. Kris always believed information should be shared on a need-to-know basis. "Andres, Alex, and the rest of the workers in the bunkhouses were spared."

"Where is Guerrero now?"

"I have no idea." She'd been racking her brain trying to figure out their next move.

"Guerrero's too invested to leave the area overnight. Money, weapons, privacy," he ticked off. "Everything's at his fingertips." Kris's voice trailed off when she shook her head. "Hell, just what he's got hidden in the caves overlooking the ranch would buy up half the state."

"They're gone. Dr. Treviño took Guerrero and left town." Monica assured him. "So what happens now?"

"We're trying to piece the information together." Kris pressed his lips together, retreating into his thoughts.

"The propane tank behind the house exploded," she prodded, refusing to let him go silent.

"Yes. We have at least seven guards dead, along with two live-ins. The number may be higher. Some of the men Guerrero sent out may have returned."

She sucked in a breath. So many lives. At least three of them from outside the cartel. He exhaled. "How did this guy go from the bunkhouse to the main house without getting noticed? That doesn't make sense."

"He made it into the house?"

"Our bugs picked up a lot of movement before the explosion, but nothing to indicate who was moving around."

Moni sank onto the bed. She'd learned long ago that Kris looked at things from every angle, making sure everything fit before drawing conclusions.

"Something happened with one of the women."

Moni pulled up her knees. "What do you mean? I thought only Lourdes and Maria lived in the house, and they weren't cartel." Dr. Treviño hadn't mentioned anyone else. But then he'd never tell her if Guerrero brought home women to sleep with.

Her gaze shot to him. If they had the house bugged, he knew about Susana. Kris's penetrating look made her insides shrink into a tiny knot. Lord, he knew who the woman was, and why she was there. Moni cringed inwardly. He also knew Andres had been coming from her own bedroom... Why couldn't the ground open up and swallow her right about now?

Kris's face didn't give anything away. "One of them found something. The other one was adamant she tell someone."

"Wh-What did she find?"

"We don't know. When Damian set up the devices, he was aiming to catch Guerrero talking, not the help. We only got a snippet of their conversation."

Damian. She bit her lip. She'd had a moment of doubt when Simon talked about the body being found. Should she ask? Somehow voicing a doubt seemed so disloyal. If the cover story was put out, she heard what she was supposed to.

Andres couldn't be mixed up in the murders...could he? She didn't want him to be, but he'd talked about getting rid of them, a few at a time. Now, with the fire, Guerrero had left, and he had the ranch back. And a family of his own he hadn't mentioned. What about the times his vocabulary slipped and he forgot to act like the cowboy he claimed to be? He was the owner's son. Why hide his education? She sighed. He was a puzzle she'd never get to unravel. She swallowed the guilt, the tears, and the pain. It was time to move on.

"How is Damian?" she asked in a hollow voice.

"He's coming along. Doing PT and giving his therapist a hard time." He shook his head in disgust.

The nagging splinter of concern fell away. The rumors about Damian's death were nothing more than a cover story to keep him safe. Good enough for even her to have wondered.

Her heart constricted in her hollowed-out chest. "Let's head to the kitchen," she said, eager to escape his all-seeing eyes.

"What's wrong?"

She managed a smile as she led them across the apartment. "I'm free to go back to Monterrey." She gave an exaggerated sigh. "Finally."

"Monterrey, huh?" It wasn't until now that she realized she hadn't thought about this move as going *home*. "I thought you were hell-bent on coming here. Now that Guerrero's gone you could set pretty good roots."

After everything, she couldn't imagine staying here. Not after Andres. She waved her hand around to encompass the town. "This place is decades behind the rest of the world. I'm practically a walking scandal just because I live alone. Can you imagine?" She went to the fridge for two soft drinks, setting them on the table. "Besides, it was only temporary, until I heard from Dr. Chavez."

Kris took a seat and popped off the lids on the glass bottles. "And?"

"He called this morning. The job is mine if I want it...but if...I leave, they won't have adequate medical care nearby." Her nerves stretched thin. She hadn't thought this through. Coming to the kitchen meant sitting down face-to-face with Kris. "I don't know if Dr. Treviño will be available anytime soon. Guerrero is in a bad way, and he may end up more cloistered than before. And really, could you see anyone jumping for joy to set up practice here?"

Kris nodded, giving her a pensive look before his features hardened. "So Andres has nothing to do with whatever's tearing you up?"

Even though she'd expected the topic, his question was still a slap in the face. Exhaustion, stress, and pain threatened to crumble her façade. She folded her arms across her stomach. Kris interrogated people for a living. Hiding anything from him would be impossible. "I'm not ready for that question yet," she managed to whisper.

"Fair enough." He drank from the bottle then inhaled, letting his shoulders settle. "When you're ready, you know I'll be here."

Tears pooled in her eyes. "I just need a little time." She sniffed, grabbing a napkin from the holder at the table.

"Then we're back to Chavez. What are you going to tell him?"

"Lord, I don't know." For so long her focus had been to work with Monterrey's new ambulatory group. They supported the emergency rooms at several hospitals, taking the surplus head count, mostly victims of cartel violence.

If she could save one little boy from what Kris had suffered... She could still remember his shattered expression when her parents brought him home. He and his parents had been caught in the crossfire of a cartel execution. His mother—her aunt—had shielded him, keeping him alive.

"How about you take my reservation in Monterrey, so you can think this out?" He reached into his pocket, returning with a keycard. "Now that I know you're safe I can get home before my wife knows I'm in Mexico without her."

She laughed into the napkin. "Awww, is my big, bad, gun-toting cousin scared of his petite little wife?"

"I'm cautiously concerned," he grumbled. She fell back laughing and wiped her nose.

"How is Tessa?"

A smile spread along his lips, and his face softened, transforming him into a younger self. "Pregnant." She pressed steepled hands on either side of her nose as her eyes welled up all over again. "Yep, you're going to be an aunt."

She smiled through the tears. Both would finally have the family they'd missed out on. Any baby Tessa and Kris made was sure to be beautiful. Red-haired little girl? Blue-eyed little boy?

Nothing could make her happier... So why did she still hurt so badly?

The last of the sun's rays cast long shadows from generations of gravestones surrounding him. Hat in hand, Andres stared down at the narrow bundles wrapped in his best sheets. Green, Maria's favorite color. At least he'd send her off in something she would have surrounded herself with in life.

He dragged in a breath, running a sooty sleeve across his brow. How long had he stood there, unable to say a final good-bye to the women he'd grown up with?

Maria constantly tried to feed him because "a man needed good food to grow." When he'd gone off to school, he'd missed her cooking the most. Not that he'd ever admit such a thing to his mother, who was sure he'd miss the family.

Mom had hired Lourdes to clean and do laundry when he was about ten. She'd started giving Maria a hand in the kitchen which usually led to them bickering. Sometimes to the extent where Maria would chase her out of the kitchen with a big metal spoon in hand.

Lourdes's laughter echoed in his memory, pulling at his lips. The woman had a knack for finding out all his secrets. Her first week she'd dug up the magazine stash he'd kept hidden from Mom for years—and she'd never let him forget it, though she'd never ratted him out.

His smile faded. They didn't deserve to die like this. Had they suffered? If God was merciful, they hadn't felt a thing. His chest tightened. After the fire burned itself out he'd carried enough buckets of water from the river to drown any embers in his path. He'd cut through a hill of damp rubble until he'd found the women's charred remains, still on their mattresses. As far as he could tell they'd died in their sleep.

Had Guerrero double-crossed someone? Pissed off the wrong guy? The person doing this, or sending someone, had a lot of anger against Guerrero. Why else go after his daughter in such a brutal manner? The killer had targeted Guerrero and his people. Lourdes and Maria were collateral damage. If they'd been out to get everyone, they would have burned all the buildings. His place included.

Rayo snorted from his spot under a nearby tree. In the distance, a dust cloud stretched along the main road. Andres adjusted his hat then jammed the shovel into the dirt he'd unearthed. "They won't come close enough to notice I didn't brush your coat today." The horse turned, slapping his tail around in annoyance. "If they did, I'm sure they'd understand."

Vehicles had been driving along the road for hours. But even the most curious didn't venture past the fence line. The driver in the beat-up gray Chevy would be no different. Andres watched him out of the corner of his eye. The truck slowed to a crawl as he passed the turnoff. Just long enough for the dust to funnel around him, then he sped up.

He shot Rayo an exhausted look. "Told ya." Much as he wanted to ignore the thought of the last car to pull into the drive, he couldn't. "Damn woman." She'd headed straight for the ranch, knowing the place was on fire. "Not a lick of sense," he muttered. He still couldn't figure out if he'd been pissed at her or annoyed that she'd put herself in danger. Regardless, physical labor had a way of purging the pissiness straight out of a guy.

She'd been in true ice princess mode, but she'd looked pale, and her eyes were big and worried—over him? But why? She'd had her fling with the hired help. Now she could go back to the oversized hulk of a man and pretend what they had together never happened. It didn't matter that she'd cut through all the bullshit he'd surrounded himself in or that she'd understood the life he'd chosen, and for a few hours he'd hoped for something more, even if she hadn't.

When he'd gotten back to the ranch, everything was eerily still. He'd taken in the destruction, afraid something happened while he was away. But no, everyone just cleared out. Probably figuring if Guerrero was gone, they'd be free to leave, too. He couldn't blame them. No one would want to live with a terrorist lurking in the night.

With no one else left, and no law to speak of, he'd cleared the bodies alone. The fire went on for hours, until there was nothing left to burn. A lump rose in his throat, cutting off his breath. Lord, the smell of burned flesh would stay with him forever.

He'd gathered what he could find of the night guards' remains while waiting for the fire to die down. Later, he'd figure out where to bury the men in the bunkhouse. But there was no way in hell he'd put Guerrero's men in the family cemetery alongside his grandfather. Maybe he'd go up into the mountains and find a cave with a deep chasm. He stabbed the dirt with particular aggression, knowing, despite his venting, he'd give them a decent burial even without the benefit of a priest's blessing.

Sweat rolled down his temples in fat drops. He ran the crook of his arm across his face and kept going, unwilling to stop even for some much-needed water.

His eyes burned, and his back hurt, but he'd see the women buried before nightfall. Tomorrow he'd track down the priest and have him come out to say a few words so their souls could rest in peace.

Chapter Twelve

"You make damn good coffee."

Andres let the screen door slam behind him, cursing himself for not taking the gun Alex had left him. A mountain of a man sat at the table, a cup in his massive hand. The same hand that had been clamped around Andres's throat yesterday.

"Glad you like it." It wasn't hard to figure out what the guy wanted with him, but he'd sure like to know how he'd gotten in his house without the dogs barking a warning.

Granite features studied him for a second before he pushed away from the table. Andres stiffened, wondering how much of a beating he was going to endure from the guy towering over him by a good foot or so. And whether or not he could get some hits in. "I'm Angel. You may have heard of me through Damian." The giant stretched out a hand. "Or Monica," he added with a hint of a smile.

Andres stuck out his hand slowly. Caution warred with a strong desire to wipe the smile off his face with a well-placed fist. As he studied him, he recognized the jealousy streaking through him, though he'd never felt such a vicious clawing at his gut before.

"Sorry to show up unannounced, but with both of them gone, I had nobody to bring me by."

"How's Damian do—" The statement sank in, freezing his words. She was gone? Without even… He shut his mouth. The question about Damian lost to the unexpected news. Of course she was gone—why would she stay? His gaze searched Angel's face, thinking back to the smile her name had produced.

"—wanted to come by and check on you." Andres snapped back, realizing he'd missed part of what the guy said.

"I'm alive." He pushed past the agony carving out a piece of his chest and tried to focus on the here and now. "Which is more than I can say for most of the people who'd been living here."

"I wanted to ask you a couple questions about what happened."

Angel headed to the coffeepot with the cup he'd grabbed earlier. "I'd hoped you'd have some insight on what happened. We can't figure out who's on the hunt, but it seems pretty obvious the cartel is the sole target. At the moment, none of our intel from the other groups has anything on Guerrero or his location."

"I only set trackers in the trucks they used pretty much every day." Andres glanced at Angel. "There wasn't one in the truck they ended up taking when they left."

Angel stared into his coffee. "Luck of the devil. Nobody ever sees them coming or going."

"Nobody saw the ghost, either, yet he killed over a dozen people within days." Andres reached for a coffee cup, his back protesting after the abuse he'd taken yesterday.

"Yeah, one of those was mine." Angel's face went hard.

Andres swore under his breath. "I didn't know. I took

them up the mountain, buried them as best I could."

Angel exhaled. "Nobody will come looking for him." Andres couldn't imagine being so alone. Even when he'd been away he'd known his mother worried about him. "He'd cut ties with everyone when he signed up. Working on the inside had become his life."

As he reached for the pot to pour himself a cup, he saw Angel's phone. The screen showed a picture of him with Monica, both in formals. She was tucked into his side, joy evident in every beautiful feature. Andres tightened his grip on the handle, forcing himself not to snap it in half.

"You okay?" Angel tilted the cup back, watching him over the rim.

"Yeah," Andres croaked out. Angel had no right to reach past the wall of animosity he'd set firmly between them. He'd gotten the girl and walked away the winner. Andres sucked it up. No need for the bastard to know how much it hurt inside to admit that, even just to himself.

Seconds ticked by. Why didn't he get on with it? Why was he so damn cordial after finding his woman with another man?

Angel settled against the counter, and Andres could feel the weight of his gaze on him. "You asked about Damian. I figured you'd ask about Monica, too."

Smug bastard. "He left here hurt."

"So did she."

His head snapped back at the calm words. "What happened? Is she okay?"

Calculating eyes stared back at him. Despite his calm appearance, Angel had a lot going on inside. Maybe he should be worried, but right now getting an answer about Monica was more important.

"She was all broken up, and I intend to find out why."

Andres glared at him, incredulous. "Maybe that's

something you should take up with her. As far as I knew, she was single. We had a thing, and now it's done. You told me yourself she left, so if you want details, you need to get them from her."

Andres defiantly held Angel's gaze. No matter what Monica had done, he wasn't going to tell anyone what had happened with her. Those memories were his alone. If Angel wanted to beat the story outta him he was more than welcome to try. *I know I can't win, you prick, but I can damn sure leave a mark or two you'll have to explain when you get home.*

"I'm not sure she should settle for a man who won't fight for her."

What? Andres's lip curled. *The son of a bitch had no idea...* Clenching his fists, he took a step when Angel held up his hand.

"We're blood relatives, Moni and I."

Andres stopped and rocked back on his heels. For once, the guy didn't look like he was etched out of stone.

"She's my cousin by birth, and my sister by circumstance."

Well, that was nowhere near what he'd expected. The band around his chest gave way a little.

"Thank you for looking out for her." Angel's tone lowered, as if he wasn't used to the expression.

"Yeah, I did a fuckin' great job, huh? You sure didn't have any problem sneaking up on me."

"I figure you're allowed to fuck up once." The unspoken consequence hung in the air between them.

"If you're her blood, why the hell would you send her out here with all the shit going on?"

Angel scoffed. "I didn't send her out here. That damn mule-headed female does whatever the she sets her mind to." He shrugged. "I made full use of the opportunity and kept eyes on her as best I could." He went back to his coffee. "Now that we've got that out of the way, what are your intentions here?"

Fuck. Until thirty seconds ago he didn't know intentions were an option. "I shoulda found a way to talk to her. Explained—" He didn't even know what he'd be apologizing for. He could think of a few ways he'd fucked up, but the scene in her apartment wasn't one of them.

He glanced over at Angel. "Why the big secret about you two? Why didn't she just tell me straight out?"

Angel sized him up and seemed to come to a decision. Carefully putting the cup down, he crossed his arms over his chest. "The cartel has a bounty on me. No matter what her feelings are for you, she would never say or do anything that might lead them to me." He quirked an eyebrow at Andres. "It's an admirable trait that I greatly appreciate."

Andres blew out a breath. How could he fault the guy after his own dealings with the cartel? Angel was one of the good guys, and damn if his attitude toward the son of a bitch wasn't thawing out.

"I don't even know if it'll make a difference at this point, even if I get her to listen. This is my home. It's been my family's land for six generations. Getting it back has been all I've thought about…everything I've worked for."

"And Moni?"

Shit. His throat tightened. Before Monica, everything had been for his family's land. Now, hell, he would give it away to have her.

He could so easily see her in his life, and he in hers. He pushed the words past his lips. "She was pretty clear from the start she was never gonna stay here."

"So where does that leave you?"

"Caught between heaven and hell." Andres gave him a grin he didn't feel.

Angel stepped forward. "Let's try this again." He held out his hand. "Kristopher Angel Harmon. Kris."

Andres took the outstretched hand. "Andres Calderon, of Rancho del Sol."

"Well Andres Calderon…" Angel grinned at him. "Of Rancho del Sol…the decision is yours at this point." Releasing his grip, he grabbed his cup and placed it by the sink. "But if the tables were turned, Moni's the type of woman who'd crawl through hell on her hands and knees to get to you." He pulled an envelope out of his pocket, setting it on the table before walking out the door without a backward glance, just as silently as he seemed to do everything else.

Andres's brow creased as he picked it up and turned it over. It was blank, but he could feel something inside. Opening it, he found a single sheet of paper, folded in half, with a name and address written on it. The pain of loss and heartache eased for the first time in days.

Life was giving him a second chance, and not just with the ranch.

Andres leaned against a scarred desk at the police station. With Guerrero gone Mario had returned and agreed to take over the chief's position for the time being. Now he stood next to Andres as they both stared at the body lying on the bottom bunk of the jail cell. Mario shook his head, a deep-set frown on his face. "So this Carlo guy was masquerading as one of their own?"

"I guess." Andres shrugged.

"Why did he start shooting?" Mario held his gaze.

"I don't know what to tell you." Andres crossed his arms. The explanation sounded fishy, even to him, and he'd seen everything firsthand. "We were on the other side of the stable when he went off. I thought he was shooting at me. The doctor ended up caught in the middle."

"Poor old man," Mario lamented. "You're both lucky to be alive."

Andres nodded. He had to hand it to Dr. Treviño. The old man must have seen death bearing down on him. He'd been staring at Uncle Rey's memorial with something between relief and sadness. Likely glad they wouldn't need to put up a ribbon to mark his end also. Thank goodness Carlo's aim had been thrown off. A few inches and the bullet would've gone through a vital organ.

"I wouldn't have thought Carlo was the assassin."

"Same here," Andres piped in. "He musta worked for another outfit." Both men shook their heads. "Why else would he just start shooting?" The explanation made about as much sense as any other.

"You know, this didn't happen all of a sudden. The guy had been in town for over a week before I heard he showed up at the ranch."

"So he was already here during the rodeo?" Andres had been too busy staying away from people to notice Carlo hanging around.

"Oh yeah. The chief pointed him out to me days before."

Now the story made more sense. Barrios had been sniffing after someone. Could Carlo have been the one he suspected? Damn. He'd mentioned an unexpected connection. "So, you thinking about keeping the chief's badge?

Mario studied the light film of dust covering the desks. "Why? You looking for a job?"

He gave a self-deprecating laugh. "You that hard up to hire people?"

Mario scoffed, giving him a sidelong look before he sobered. "You're serious." Mario asked in disbelief.

He shook his head, tapping his fingers on the desk. "You've been helping the law for years. You shoot, rope, ride, and you're the best damn tracker in the area." Mario ticked off. "If it wasn't for your brother wanting to keep you outta danger, Barrios would have hired you years ago."

"Man, you gotta have some cojones to settle in the middle of the cartel without being one of 'em." Mario's eyes held admiration. "People respect you for that. Hell, half the town was trying to get to your place yesterday. But Ms. Lupe said the fire was under control, and Dr. Treviño sent everyone away."

He ran his hand along the back of his neck. Had he been so deep in self-doubt that he'd read things wrong? "My hands are full right now, man. Getting the ranch back in working order is gonna take time."

Mario nodded. "I've been asked if you were going to set up again."

Andres crossed one boot over the other. "It'll be a while before I can take on any stock. There's a lot of repairs that've been ignored for too long."

"Well, you got a few people interested in sending horses, if a Calderon is running the ranch." He tilted his head. "Though it's hard to imagine the place without Alex."

Andres looked thoughtful, his chest a little hollow, knowing Alex hadn't been around this morning. They'd finally made peace, but he'd still lost his lifelong friend.

Mario dragged in a deep breath. "None of my business... but I hope you two got past the whole thing with Susana." *Ah, shit.* He didn't wanna go down this road. "Her daddy knows what he raised. I think he was just pissed you were too smart to marry her. He was banking on having his whole family living in that big house." Andres set his jaw. Guerrero, Susana, and now her father. He'd never understand how ambition could warp a person. "Still, it's hard to believe Alex left town."

"He's gonna look after Dr. Treviño for a while, but he'll be back."

"Well, I wish 'em the best. I think Guerrero probably

needs to see his kid and thank the Almighty they made it out alive."

Andres struggled with a lump in his throat. Nobody knew about Paloma's gruesome end. Maybe things were best left unsaid—for everyone's sake.

"These drug wars have turned the world inside out." Mario tightened his lips. "Now you never know what the guy next to you is capable of." He huffed. "Hell, you should buy yourself some lottery tickets." Grinning, he said, "You took out a killer, saved a man's life, and came out without needing a doctor."

Andres settled back. While not all the right people made it out alive, needing a doctor had just taken on a whole new meaning for him.

He'd thought he had nothing to offer her... But maybe, even without the ranch, he could be the man she wanted. The man she needed. He looked up at Mario. "Think you can help me find someone to help with the horses?"

"Yeah." He tapped on the desk again. "You driving up to see the lady doctor?"

"Maybe." Andres narrowed his eyes.

"Figured." He laughed. "Hell, man, I was at the rodeo. You really expect *anyone* to believe you got thrown 'cause you can't handle a horse?"

Chapter Thirteen

For someone who had always known her mind, made her own decisions, and stood by them, Moni was lost. She watched the distant sunset out the window of her borrowed hotel room. She found herself longing for the spectacular colors of the sun as it slid behind the mountains outside Copas. She missed knowing the people around her. Here the mass of bodies stifled her. After spending months willing the phone to ring with her reprieve, she now found herself longing for the familiar surroundings. But she had no place in Copas anymore. She wouldn't be able to live so close to Andres without the pain of loss.

Even food held no appeal—which was enough to know something was wrong. Maybe she should try pizza and beer. It might help her get out of this funk. Because really, she couldn't hide forever. She owed Dr. Chavez a call but still had no idea what she'd tell him.

A knock at her door brought her out of her musing. Someone looking for Kris? She approached the door cautiously, knowing the danger he lived with every day.

Peering through the peephole brought her up short. She flattened her palms against the door, feeling like the world tilted on its axis.

"Monica, open the door, please." Andres knocked again.

She steeled herself and called through the door. "No. Go away."

"Please, baby, I'd rather not yell everything through the door and get myself thrown out. But I will if that's what it takes."

She dropped her forehead onto the smooth wood, knowing since he'd been able to find her it was through Kris. And the rat had probably given him a key card to use in case she was stubborn. She unlocked the door and pulled it open, motioning him in with a sharp nod. "You have thirty seconds to convince me I should listen to anything you say."

"Thank you, sweetheart." He exhaled as he stepped inside, pulling off the ever-present cowboy hat.

She closed the door and turned to face him. His fingers twisted the brim as he focused his gaze on her. "That night... my house was burning to the ground behind me, it fell to me to get Susana out of there, I was upset about Alex leaving, and worried about Dr. Treviño. The hardest part..." His hands squeezed tightly, crushing the hat. "The hardest part was believing I'd already lost you." He shook his head. "None of that is an excuse. Sometimes I do stupid shit even when I think I have good reasons for doing it."

She stared at him, his raw honesty stripping away all her misconceptions about him. Her mind raced with ways to explain her side of that night. "Andres, about Angel..."

He held up a hand. "It's okay, Kris and I talked. I understand the risk he took doing that. No matter what happens between us, Monica, you need to know I'll never, ever, compromise his safety. And as for Susana, believe me when I tell you, I was getting her out of my house and the hell off my land."

She curled her toes into the thick carpet as her mind reeled with the implications of his words. *Kris* had told Andres. It spoke volumes about what kind of man he thought Andres was.

"Her family has a small place on the other side of town. I took her home and set her father straight. Regardless of what she's done, she's still his blood."

"And the baby?" Nerves tightened her stomach as she waited for the truth.

"Her baby. Not mine. I didn't know she lied. And I guess everyone was trying to avoid calling me an asshole for abandoning my blood."

He shook his head, lines of fatigue digging in around his eyes. "I shouldn't have walked away that night. I should have told you how I felt, right then and there. I'm sorry about that. If you give me a chance, I'll spend the rest of our lives together making it up to you. I'll never give you cause to doubt me again."

He hadn't lied. Shoulders weak with relief, she welcomed the knowledge with heart-pounding hope.

She'd left, hurt and angry, judging him by what happened to her. A series of stupid misunderstandings led her to make a bad choice, one that could still be fixed. Her reasons for keeping him at a distance seemed so small and insignificant now, especially when compared to the promises she saw in his eyes. Pushing past the lump in her throat, she took a deep breath and bared her soul.

"A few days before I arrived in Copas, my mother had arranged a party to introduce my fiancé to the family. Turns out…we all got to meet his pregnant girlfriend and her two angry brothers."

He blinked, and understanding dawned on his face. "And you thought I—" He shook his head adamantly. "I'm so sorry, sweetheart." He stepped forward, and she surrendered to his embrace, letting his arms slide around her as they backed into the room. The heat of his body blanketed her in warmth and comfort. He kept murmuring apologies, his arms tightening around her until she didn't know where she ended and he began.

His scent surrounded her. And for the first time since that horrible night, she felt at peace. Like coming home after being away too long. "I couldn't stay there. Not after you... well, I thought..." She dragged in a breath.

He took her face in his hands, staring into her eyes. "Shhh, it's okay. I understand."

She sniffed, realizing something that escaped her six months ago. The pain and embarrassment had been over being taken for a fool, not over the man. Not like this time. No matter what she'd done, she hadn't been able to get Andres out of her head. This time she'd been grieving over the loss of the man she'd fallen in love with.

"Part of me wants to break that idiot in two for hurting you." He kissed the top of her head then set his forehead against hers. The lines around his tired eyes relaxed. "The other part wants to thank him for being such a douchebag. Otherwise I never would have met you."

He kissed her. Tenderly. So much that it brought tears to her eyes. "Tell me about her. All of it. I don't want any more surprises."

He drew her against his shoulder. "Susana was a pretty girl. Well liked. She probably had too many guys chasing after her." He exhaled. "When I came back from college we... bumped into each other in town. She started up a conversation and... well, she'd always been kinda quiet around me. Figured she'd grown up while I was gone."

"We saw each other over the next few weeks. My mother wasn't exactly thrilled. Dad thought I was 'sowing wild oats.'" Something in his tone made her think his dad's comments had been more graphic. "The cartel stuff started getting pretty bad. She was scared and wanted to get out. I couldn't help it. The feeling of…being a protector got to me." He sighed. "My parents had a fit. They wanted me to start my master's—"

"Wait, your master's?"

"Computer science degree with a math minor." She tilted her head, arching her eyebrow. He gave an answering shrug. "It was my parents' dream. Not mine."

"It wasn't until she and I were leaving that I found out she'd been seeing Alex." A tired breath escaped. "We got into it. Words were said. Choices were made. I got the hell out."

Moni nodded, understanding the ever present tension between the two friends.

"Getting Susana smuggled into the States pretty much emptied my bank account. I couldn't go to my dad for money, not after how things went down. And my damn pride wouldn't let me go to Rudy or Brianna, my brother and sister. In school they tell you people are gonna throw money at you hand over fist. But reality was *nothing* like that. The U.S. economy was at an all-time low. I couldn't find a job. Couldn't support us. Couldn't go back to school. With no real world experience, my BA was just an expensive piece of paper. I ended up a day laborer."

"Did you ever think of coming back?" she asked.

"Yeah. A lot. But never more than when she told me she was pregnant." He shook his head. "We had a room in a place we shared with five other people. She wanted more, so she started cleaning houses to earn some money and found someone who could give her a better life. By the time I got back, Guerrero had taken over the ranch, and my parents and siblings were living in California."

"Have you spoken to them?"

"Briefly," he said with a faraway note in his voice.

"I think you've spent too much time beating yourself up over this."

He focused on a spot high on the wall. "I felt really stupid. Maybe…I guess I still do." She tightened her arms around him. "For letting myself get taken in when pretty much *everyone* told me what she was about."

"They're growing pains. Things you have to go through yourself because nobody could possibly understand."

"The experience certainly made me grow up." A brief, humorless smile touched his lips.

"You talked to Alex?"

"Yes."

"And he still left?"

"For a while. He had a few things to work out." She could understand that. Life had taken a few unexpected turns for all of them in a short time. Andres brushed his lips against her temple. "And you, baby? Are you working through a few things?"

She lay her head against his chest, right over his heart. The strong, steady beat echoed in her ear. "Dr. Treviño sent me back. Then Dr. Chavez called with a job offer." The job was hers, if she wanted it. She should be wanting to high-five everyone in the building, yet she felt nothing remotely resembling excitement.

"I guess congratulations are in order," he murmured.

She gently pushed him back to create space between them. "Your thirty seconds are up, cowboy."

He swallowed hard, looking down and nodding slightly.

"So I guess I'll have to give you another few minutes to hear the rest of what you have to say."

She barely had the words out of her mouth when he tossed his hat to the side and snaked his arms around her, picking her up off the floor. She held on tight, wrapping her legs around him.

He kissed her, his tongue sweeping past her lips. She dug her fingers into his hard shoulders and her bare heels into the backs of his thighs. Cupping her bottom, he stumbled away from the wall as she tore at the buttons on his shirt. Somehow they made it to the bed and fell on it, wound around each other. He broke the kiss and lifted his head to look deep into her eyes.

"I love you, Monica, and I'm not going to lose you if I can help it. But it has to be your choice."

Tears stung her eyes.

"I need you in my life," he said in a voice roughened by raw emotion. "In my home. And yes." He cupped her breast. "In my bed."

"I love you, too." She blinked back tears but didn't manage to stop them all.

"Don't cry, sweetheart." His lips pressed against her temple. "Tomorrow morning we can go talk to your parents, then we'll start looking for a place."

Her stomach flip-flopped. "But your ranch."

"We don't have to go back." He brushed her cheek with such tenderness. "Mario agreed to look after the horses until I can find someone to do it full time."

"You waited so long to have your life back. That ranch is your heart."

His beautiful eyes went soft. "I thought so once, but I was wrong. You're my heart, and I've waited even longer to find you. I can live with visiting the ranch. But I could never live without you."

Time stood still, just long enough for everything to become clear to her. Leaving Copas, and the ranch, seemed like a loss for her, too. Going back, opening the office, helping people who would really need her, and most importantly, settling in with Andres sent her spirit racing. She cupped his jaw and pulled his face down to hers. "Aren't you lucky you won't have to live without either one," she murmured against his lips, just before she kissed him.

Epilogue

Moni smiled. The heat of Andres's kiss lingered on her lips, stirring dirty thoughts. Rayo took careful steps away from the front porch. Although her husband complained about the horse's superior attitude, they'd remained inseparable since she'd come to live at the ranch. Rayo understood Andres's moods, including the pride with which he rode today. In his arms, a tiny fist pushed away the blue blanket, trying to see the ranch as every Calderon should—from horseback.

Their son was the first new Calderon of his generation at Rancho del Sol. He had acres of land to learn about, generations' worth of history, and a benevolent spirit who kept watch over the stables.

Rancho del Sol was up and running thanks to some of the money hidden away in nearby caves. Once the repairs were done, they'd opened shop. With stables full and well-tended, the stock was in demand for races and stud fees.

Most importantly, Andres had his legacy back, along with his father's respect, and they were continuing their life together — as a family.

The Calderons of Rancho del Sol.

Acknowledgements

Thank you to Ria Boulay, the best crit partner an author could ask for. Thank you for all the hard work you did filling in blanks and fixing words to have Andres and Moni's story ready in time.

Thank you Linda, Kri, and Fred Madrigal for clearing up the medical questions.

Nancy Gonzalez, Greet Gatlin, Dave Bowen, thanks for the extra time to do last minute edits.

To Letti, Danny, Nana, Mike, Chags, and Brat, thanks for your support and understanding when I disappeared to work on my manuscript or had my nose in a book. By the way, this was the best vacation EVER!!!

About the Author

Sahara Roberts caught the writing bug early in life. She enjoys writing Romantic Suspense and Contemporary Romance. Her days are filled with international trade issues (the legal kind) and her evenings writing steamy romance.

Sahara lives in South Texas with her husband and two spoiled cats.

Discover the **Dangerous Desires** *series...*

Desire & Deception

Deep cover agent Kris Harmon walks a tight line between vicious drug runners with agendas of their own and working with the cartel leaders he's trying to organize. Any distraction could prove fatal. When Tessa Marshal is mistaken for a drug mule and taken captive, time runs out for both of them, Tessa has to reach beyond her fears and trust a stranger while Kris must choose between his lifelong ambitions and saving Tessa's life. If they want to survive, both must trust that there is more to the other than what meets the eye.